05/09

17 AUG

DEMON
STALKERS

TORMENT

Also available by Douglas Hill

DEMON STALKERS: PREY

Coming soon

DEMON STALKERS: VENGEANCE

For my granddaughter Aoife

1

He was just a bundle of rags huddled against a wall. I barely glanced at him.

But then, by chance, I had a glimpse of him turning to watch me. And smiling. A smile full of malice and cruelty and evil triumph.

I'd seen that smile before.

And I knew that all the terror was about to start again.

I'd been hurrying along a busy street in the northern part of the city, through a dank early-December afternoon. It wasn't easy to hurry, since the pre-Christmas spending craziness was well under way and the pavements were packed with slow-moving shoppers. Window shoppers, mostly. I've noticed that most of the actual *spending* at that early stage isn't on gifts so much as on stocks of booze, to kick-start the ho-ho Christmas cheer.

Christmas is really for kids, I think, since they can

be naturally cheerful. If they're lucky. But if they're not . . .

I had never got – or given – a Christmas present in my life.

My boozy mother spent what money she had in pubs, and probably never even knew when the season came around. After she died I was on my own, a homeless kid on the streets, surviving on the fringes of what people call normal life. Getting gifts was as alien to me as learning Martian.

But that Christmas was different. I'd been out during the day doing odd jobs for stallholders I vaguely knew in a street market. Earning a bit of cash, not just for food but maybe, for once, for a present.

For the friend who'd come into my life, putting an end to loneliness. For April.

She was working too, in the kitchen of a side-street cafe. There are always people who'll pretend to believe that we're over sixteen and give us work, because we can't complain when they pay us badly.

In fact April is probably around fourteen, though she doesn't know for sure. And I'm fourteen too – which I definitely know.

I've been fourteen for years.

We had just got back to the city a few days earlier. We'd been in the depths of the country – not by choice – and coming back had taken a while. You don't travel quickly when you have no money.

And though April probably could have taken all the cash out of any bank without getting caught, she flatly refused to steal anything, ever.

You don't live well, either, when your pockets are empty. We hadn't gone to any of the city's charity shelters, since they would have separated us. So we ended up squatting in a derelict house full of damp and mould and mice and probably a few rats. But we didn't plan to stay there for long, and both of us had known worse.

'It's better than sleeping in doorways,' April had said when we found the place.

She'd lived on the streets too, not as long as me but long enough.

'Probably,' I'd said. 'Though some place warmer would be good.'

She'd laughed. 'A room at the Ritz?' But then her big hazel eyes went serious. 'At least this is safer than the streets, Nick. And it won't be too cold.'

She was right, of course. Though she might feel differently after a heavy frost or two in the depths of winter. I couldn't ever get sick, but she could.

So I was weaving through the crowds that afternoon, jingling newly earned cash in my pocket, wondering if we could afford a cheap youth hostel for a night or two – not long enough to draw attention to ourselves or start anyone asking questions. I was also wondering if we should get curry or Chinese for supper.

And when I first glanced at the ragged beggar on the corner, I thought idly that he'd be jingling some cash too. He was doing well, plenty of coins bouncing into the greasy cap on the pavement by his feet.

I suppose people dropped their Christmas-kindly coins because they felt sorry for him. He was thin and hunched and grubby, with dirty white hair straggling down to his shoulders. And he was standing with the help of rickety, old-fashioned wooden crutches, and metal braces on his lower legs.

I didn't expect him even to look at me. Beggars don't ask street kids for spare change. But as I got past him and stopped at the kerb, waiting for a break in the traffic, I saw his reflection in the wing mirror of a parked van.

He had straightened up, on his crutches, and was staring after me. With that evil, gleeful, *giveaway* smile.

The last time I'd seen that smile, it had been on the bony face of a sadistic sorcerer named Fray, who was having fun slicing and dicing my flesh with more magical flying knives than I could count.

2

I didn't look around or give any sign that I'd spotted him. I just dodged past the big van, so I was hidden from him, and drew from its sheath at my hip the knife that no ordinary person can see.

Its double-edged blade was tinged with bright gold. The glow probably would have been brighter if I was closer to the beggar. But it was confirmation enough that I was right about him.

I dashed across the street, dodging cars, getting a few angry honks and shouts from the drivers. But snarling at myself instead of them.

Not so long before, I'd had a chance to put an end to Fray, to finish him off when he was already half dead. But I hadn't been able to kill him in cold blood. Anyway, I'd been sure that he was going to manage to die all by himself.

Bad mistake. He was alive. And in one piece – because, with his powers, the crutches and leg braces had to be part of the beggar disguise. And he'd come looking for April and me.

On our way to the city, April and I had travelled in blissful peace, meeting no dangers at all. In that quiet time we guessed that our enemies were busy clearing up and reorganizing after what we'd done. And we aimed to keep our heads down and make the lull last as long as possible.

But now, a lot sooner than we'd hoped, we were being stalked again.

So no more mistakes, I told myself. And we wouldn't be just running, as I'd done so often before. There didn't seem much point in running, anyway, from an evilly powerful sorcerer who had located me in one of the world's most crowded cities.

But also, things were different now. April and I together could keep ourselves safer than I'd ever managed on my own. And maybe, I thought, we might even find a way to deal with Fray if – when – he came after us.

Turn and stalk the stalker, I said to myself. I'd done that before too.

The knife's glow soon shifted back to its usual silver as I put distance between myself and my enemy. But I kept it in my hand anyway, so I could check its blade as I raced through alleys and along backstreets. It was a slightly longer route, but I moved faster once I got away from the crowded shopping streets. And it was mazy enough to slow down anyone trying to track me.

All along the way the knife stayed silvery and I saw no one and nothing that looked suspicious. So I'd started to relax a little by the time I reached the house.

It was in a short terrace, most of it looking ready to fall down even though some buildings still seemed to be occupied. The place we were staying had a damaged roof and boarded-up windows, but the main room on the ground floor was more or less intact. At least it kept out the wind and rain, if not the cold.

April was there before me – small and slim in jeans and a charity-shop fleece, her long, glossy chestnut hair the brightest thing in the room.

But she was standing stiffly against the peeling plaster of one wall, looking tense and troubled.

Because we had visitors. Not invited, and not welcome.

Three older boys, probably in their late teens. Hooded jackets, jeans, heavy boots, shaved heads that looked like lumpy doorknobs with ears.

The one looming in front of April was the biggest and ugliest, with a spotty, meaty face and blunt features crammed into the middle of it. He was even uglier just then, twisting his face to look threatening. His mates, one tall and bony and the other tall and porky, were grinning as their leader snarled at April.

Three big louts menacing one small girl. It wasn't fair.

They had no idea how unfair.

'You gotta have a phone,' the big one was saying as I stepped into the room. 'Everybody's got one. Maybe we'll jus' take them jeans offa you, check the pockets . . .'

Then it registered, a bit late, that someone had come in behind them. They all turned, but when they saw me they relaxed.

'Who's this, then, yer boyfriend?' the big one said to April. 'Come to save you, has he?'

The other two chortled, watching eagerly as he stamped towards me. I sheathed the knife, since I don't use it against ordinary people, and waited. Unnoticed by the thugs, April stepped away from the wall, raising one small closed fist and giving me a meaningful look.

I'm no mind reader, but we knew each other pretty well by then. I was fairly sure I knew what she meant.

'*You* better have a phone, or somethin' worth takin',' the big one growled as he reached out a beefy hand towards me.

I slid aside, dodging the hand. Then I hit him.

It wasn't a punch, more like a sweeping backhand smack. I was shorter and a lot lighter than him, and I knew that even my best punch, let alone a slap, would barely make him blink.

But I also thought I knew what was going to happen. And I was right.

As my hand whacked against the thug's heavy jaw, he was violently flung across the room towards one of the boarded-up windows. Smashing through the boards, ripping them away from the window frame, he crashed heavily down on to the pavement outside in a shower of splinters.

The other two went white, frozen for an instant with wide-eyed, open-mouthed shock. Then as I took a step towards them, hands raised, they whirled and scrambled wildly for the door. I heard their terrified gabble outside as they dragged their stunned leader away as fast as they could.

I turned to April, laughing quietly. I'd laughed more in the few weeks with her than in the whole of my life before.

'You came in at the right time,' she said. 'They followed me from the bus – and I was worried about using PK too openly.'

'So you made me look like a kung-fu master instead,' I said.

'It should make them think,' April said, 'before they go robbing other kids.'

They'd probably start robbing old ladies instead, I

9

thought, but I didn't say so. 'I wish you hadn't broken the window though,' I said, teasing. 'Now it'll be even colder in here.'

'I'll fix it after dark,' she said, 'when no one can see.'

She didn't mean night-time DIY. She would put new boards back on the window in the same way that she had flung the thug through it. Magically.

But not with what mages call the 'higher' magic, using spells and power objects and all that. April's magic was *psychic* – mental powers like ESP, psycho-kinesis – or PK – moving things with the mind and so on.

She was probably the most powerful psychic I'd ever met or heard about. Not a good choice of victim for muggers.

'We could use the broken boards to make a little fire,' she went on, 'if we could find a metal bucket or something to make it in.'

'As long as we keep it well hidden,' I said, getting serious. 'And ourselves. Because I just ran into someone we know . . . Mr Fray.'

She went pale and tense, as I knew she would. And with the December twilight gathering spookily around us, we perched on the old mattresses that were the half-ruined room's only furniture and talked about what to do.

It wasn't only Fray's reappearance that worried us.

He was high up in an evil organization of sorcerers, which a friend once said was like a magical Mafia. They called themselves the Cartel, and they were devoted to crime, power-seeking and vileness of every sort.

And at least some of them were devoted to finding April and me too.

They'd been after us separately long before either of us knew the other existed. But because of what April and I had done a few weeks earlier, they – or anyway Fray – would now be hunting us even more tirelessly.

Probably they still wanted to enslave April, as they always had. To make her powers serve them.

Me, they just wanted to kill.

3

It had all begun years before, just after my actual fourteenth birthday, when I had stumbled into the presence of a woman named Manta. She had red-gold hair and huge green eyes, she liked to wear long, bright, silken dresses – and she was a powerful and dangerous witch.

For years Manta had waged a one-witch war against the Cartel – because they had stolen something from her, something she called her 'most treasured possession'. In turn, for years, the Cartel had been hunting her. And on the night I met her, one of their hunters caught up with her.

Manta was somehow magically unable to spill blood, so she could never fight or kill her enemies. Instead, she used others to fight for her.

That night she used me.

But first she tried to improve my chances. She gave me the knife, which is always magically sharp and which glows golden when someone or something from the Cartel is near. But she did more than that.

She made me changeless.

Her magic, that spell, put the dark permanent Mark of Changelessness on my throat and affected every cell of my body. Through the years since then, I've stayed *exactly* the same fourteen-year-old Nick Walker, the same lean, dark-haired, scruffy street kid that I was on that night. I haven't aged, I haven't grown, I haven't gained or lost weight, I have never got sick.

I can be killed in lots of ways, as long as they're quick. But if I am only hurt, the injury heals and vanishes within minutes. I can't even have a haircut, since it just goes back to the way it was before.

But though never growing up and never getting sick might seem not so bad, for me it has been nothing less than a curse. Because that night, all those years ago, as Manta made her escape, I managed – with some luck – to kill the Cartel demon that had caught up with her.

After that, the Cartel started stalking me.

And they got steadily more determined about it when I kept killing other stalkers that they sent, over the next few years.

Then, when I met April, they became not just determined but obsessed. But they were even more obsessed

13

with her. They'd been hunting for her as well, long before she and I met.

I first saw her on Halloween. Earlier, in the summer, I'd been sort of rescued from the streets by a man named Paddy and his partner Julia. Paddy was a middle-aged guy with a touch of psychic ability and a fair share of ESP.

Since hooking up with them my existence had become almost settled – as much as it ever could be for the likes of me – and I even clung to the hope that I might find some non-Cartel mage who could reverse Manta's spell and make me normal again. At first I had imagined I could just take off to America or somewhere and be safe from the Cartel forever. But magical people of any sort can't leave this island country, because they – we – can't cross salt water.

So, on this particular Halloween night, Paddy and I were checking out a group of magical nasties who we suspected were up to all sorts of no good, including a planned blood sacrifice. The intended victim turned out to be April.

When I got her out and Paddy and I got her home, we learned what else she was.

At that time her mind was a mess. Some kind of inner blockage had left her with almost no memory of her past. And her psychic powers were blocked too, by a *second* strange mental barrier. But those powers

14

could break through, now and then, all by themselves, uncontrolled.

But Paddy was trying to help her, and I was getting to like her more and more, and we were having some nice times. Until I realized that I was putting April and Paddy and Julia at risk, and always would. Because the demon stalkers would just keep coming after me.

So I left – going on the run to keep myself safe and to keep them safer.

But in the end I couldn't outrun the Cartel's power. They took me prisoner, and Fray and his fellow mages began their evil tortures.

They also raided Paddy's house and captured April.

*Re*captured, really. She'd been their prisoner for a long time when she was much younger, but somehow she'd got away. Apparently they knew she was extra special, magically – and they wanted to brainwash her and corrupt her and make her one of their own. And being with me while I was being hunted had let them find her again.

So we were both prisoners of the Cartel – kept apart and tormented separately. Until I gave Fray the idea of bringing her to watch the disturbingly grisly things they were doing to me.

They'd expected that the horrific sight would tip her

over the edge and finally shatter her will and her resistance. But it didn't.

Instead, it somehow shattered one of the barriers in her mind.

Suddenly she was in full control, at last, of her incredible psychic power. Her PK blasted out and totally wrecked the place and we got safely away. Leaving a lot of Cartel mages and demons crushed and dead in the ruins.

But, unluckily, leaving Fray alive.

4

Having psychic powers could probably make you lazy, but it must be fun.

After dark that evening, April's ESP found some discarded but intact boards and her PK nailed them over the window. She also found a big empty tin that had once held cooking oil, for our fire. But she refused – as always – to use her PK to pinch something from a restaurant for our supper.

'We'll buy it,' she said firmly. 'I'm *not* going to be a psychic thief.' I wasn't all that keen on going out again, mostly because of the sleety rain outside. But soon we were back, being warmed up by an oil-scented fire and good, big curries. We both knew that Fray could find us in the house as easily as anywhere, and we decided to be extra careful that night, taking turns sleeping and keeping a lookout for surprise visitors. But though a visitor arrived, he didn't come in person.

When April took over guard duty, after midnight, I

was tired enough to get to sleep quite easily. But it wasn't a restful sleep when the nightmares came.

And it became fearful, when the worst of the bad dreams brought a pale hazy shape that formed itself into a face I knew. Fray, smiling that evil smile.

'Do you think to elude me, boy?' His voice was as thin and sharp as a winter wind. 'Do you and that vile girl believe you can *hide* from me? So foolish. Run and skulk as you wish, you will *never* escape my vengeance.'

In the dream I began to wonder if it really *was* a dream – or if he had magically got into my mind. I had some experience of getting messages via dream-visions. And I didn't think a nightmare of my own making would have included the glitter of madness in Fray's eyes, the fleck of foam at the corner of his mouth.

'I owe you and the girl much *pain*,' the dream-image went on. 'And I will pay that debt with interest, for what you did to me, for what I have become!'

The image seemed to pull back so that I was seeing all of him, thin and upright, wearing his usual dark suit. 'Remember?' he snarled. 'This illusion is how I was. But this, *this*, is how I am now!'

The image shivered – and suddenly he was leaning on the crutches that I'd seen that morning, with the metal braces holding his legs straight.

'Do you *see*?' He waved a crutch at me. 'This is what you and she did, how you left me! Maimed, crippled,

18

broken . . .' The voice grew shriller, the mad eyes wilder. 'And they would not *heal* me, would not let me heal *myself*! Claiming that I was at *fault* – for awakening the girl's powers, for the calamity that followed! So I have been punished, and derided, and *excluded* – in endless misery and anguish!'

Definitely not a dream, I thought. This was Fray himself, sending me a psychic message designed to terrify. But an even crazier Fray, foaming at the mouth over what had been done to him.

So his crutches and braces weren't part of his beggar disguise. Good, I thought. Even better if the Cartel really had punished him and chucked him out. I would have liked to wish him lots more misery and anguish. But it was his dream-message, and he was doing the talking.

'But now you will share the torment, you and that girl!' he raged. 'Her powers will be no more use against what I send than your paltry knife! She will be torn to pieces and *eaten*, and you will watch, helplessly! Nor will your changelessness save you when you in turn suffer the agony of being *devoured alive*!'

With the last shrieked words his image vanished – and I came awake with a yell of my own.

Across the room, in the dim light of the dying fire, I saw April jump, startled, and peer at me. 'Bad dream?' she asked.

'Not really a dream,' I muttered, sitting up. 'A message – from Fray.'

Even in the dimness I saw her turn pale as I told her what the sorcerer's image had said. 'He's off his head, April,' I said. 'Totally psycho. Which makes him even more dangerous.'

She nodded, frowning. 'It makes him stupid too. Why would he *warn* us? Now we'll be even more on our guard.'

'He doesn't care,' I said. 'He's too full of himself, like they all are – convinced that his power can wipe us out whatever we do. And he wants us to get terrified and panicky, waiting . . .'

'But we won't,' she said, looking determined. 'And we won't be so easy to wipe out either, whatever he sends to hunt us.'

I agreed with that. But for all our determination, neither of us got any more sleep that night.

In the morning though, with a bit of weak December sunlight, we weren't feeling much terror or panic. We were both used to being stalked, and we knew there wasn't much point in jumping at shadows.

Instead, we gathered up our few bits and pieces, planning to move on and keep moving, not staying in one place for long. No point making it easy for Fray.

'But first,' April said, 'we have to go back to Paddy's

house. And if I still don't sense any danger there, we should risk going in.'

That tightened my stomach a bit, but I knew she was right. Fray or not, it was something we had to do.

The house, Paddy's and Julia's home, meant a lot to both of us. We'd been safe and happy there, for a short while anyway. I'd learned for the first time what it was like being part of a warm and caring *family*.

Now, though, the house was empty. Because of me, Paddy and Julia were . . . gone.

But we were fairly sure that they weren't dead. April had said she had no *feeling* of them having died. And when a psychic with that much power talks about her feelings, you pay attention.

And in some ways it didn't seem completely beyond belief, for although Paddy wasn't that powerful, with only some ESP and no PK at all, he had an amazing amulet that he wore inside his shirt, and I'd seen how it had protected both him and Julia when the two of them came, hopelessly heroic, to try to rescue April and me. The owner of the place where we were held prisoner – a high-level Cartel mage named Redman, who was Fray's boss – had struck at them with a fiery magical blast, but the amulet deflected it.

And although the amulet hadn't seemed to help when Redman had worked another quick bit of evil sorcery – Paddy and Julia had disappeared – maybe it had done enough to save the two of them, which would explain April's sense that they were alive.

And although they could be anywhere, it had to be some other part of the country, for not even Redman could send Paddy across salt water. And April and I vowed to find them.

And although we had no idea where they might be, we felt sure that, wherever they were, they too would be searching for us. So Paddy's house seemed as good a place as any to start looking, even to see if he'd sent any sort of magical message.

But though we'd gone to the house a couple of times after getting back to the city, we hadn't gone in. We'd crept around outside, while April's ESP had a careful look. We knew the Cartel mages might well guess that we'd go back there, and might have set some kind of magic alarm or trap.

It was even more likely, now, that Fray might have done so. Especially if he was sending some devouring killer after us.

But still we had to go in. Paddy and Julia had risked almost certain death, or worse, when they came to help us. We were going to face whatever we had to face to try to help them.

5

Clouds had shut off the feeble sunshine by the time we set out, and the sky had turned flinty-grey and ominous. It wasn't a long way to Paddy's house, but we weren't in a hurry to fling ourselves into danger. Keeping to backstreets to avoid morning shoppers, we paused in a steamy cafe for cups of tea but didn't stay long. Neither of us felt like eating anything, and we didn't have much to say.

As we left the cafe April raised her head and stared all around, using her ESP to search for any hint of an enemy.

When she gave the all-clear, we went on, along a street with a blank warehouse wall along one side and a tall wooden fence along the other. Glancing through the fence's open gate, I saw a muddy space where a large hole was being dug for the foundation of some new building. The site was deserted, but cluttered with the usual heaps of concrete blocks and lumber and rusty metal mesh.

In the next instant, the street ahead of us *wasn't* deserted. April was going to need to keep her ESP switch on permanently. In front of us stood Fray. Now with shiny new metal crutches and leg braces, but still wearing his crazy-eyed grin.

I saw April's eyes flicker as if she was using PK on him, but nothing happened. That was scary – and so was Fray, as he bared his pointed teeth and lurched towards us. We whirled together and raced for the building site, where the concrete blocks and things would make useful weapons for April.

But when we heard the big gate crash shut behind us, we glanced back. The gate had not only shut but had become part of the solid fence. We saw no openings anywhere, and the fence had become higher and slippery-smooth, impossible to climb.

Much worse, it wasn't Fray that had come into the site with us.

And when we saw what it was, we nearly screamed.

A giant worm-thing – sickly white and glistening, its segmented body enormously long and thick. Its front end was mostly mouth, filled with overlapping rows of glinting saw-teeth. With snaky tendrils, probably antennae, waving and writhing around the opening.

As it came at us, hunching swiftly along caterpillar-style, April's PK effortlessly picked up a mass of the

24

metal mesh and hurled it at the monster. But the metal simply bounced off the creature, as if it was wearing invisible armour.

'Shielded,' April muttered. 'Like Fray was.'

Of course Fray would have a painfully clear memory of what April could do. So he'd magically protected himself and his creature against her power.

But still she tried again. Her PK pounded the worm with a heavy wooden beam, but it splintered and broke. She dropped the entire pile of concrete blocks on to the slimy back, but they fell away as the mesh had.

And the thing kept coming.

'Time to run,' I said, backing away, knife in hand. 'Can you PK us both over the fence?'

'I don't know,' she said. 'Fray has put some kind of barrier . . .'

But she didn't finish. The worm-monster's head lifted slightly – and spat a stream of foul liquid at her.

And though I was quick enough to slam my hand against her shoulder, I didn't quite manage to push her out of the way.

The liquid struck her on that shoulder, some splashing across my forearm.

It burned like acid or molten metal, but that wasn't all. My right arm – thankfully, as I'm left-handed – went limp and lifeless, paralysed.

But April had been hit with more of the liquid. She

crumpled, half fainting with pain, her whole left side drooping and immobilized.

And the monster lunged towards her, terrible mouth gaping.

With my agonized right arm flopping, I threw myself in front of her, stabbing at the monstrosity. The blade only glanced off the magic shielding, but the creature seemed to draw back from the knife's glow, trying to veer around me.

Fray's dream-image had said that April was to be killed first. And the worm seemed programmed for that plan, its grisly mouth reaching for her hungrily.

Hunger, I thought. *Devouring.*

In the next microsecond, with the changelessness reviving my paralysed arm, I saw a way to draw that monstrous hunger away from April.

I stabbed at the worm-thing again, to keep it back. Then I slashed with the knife in a different direction.

Downward. So that the bright blade sliced off the little finger of my right hand.

Fumbling, almost dropping the knife, I managed to catch the finger as it fell. '*Devour this!*' I yelled at the monster – and threw the bleeding fragment of my flesh into the air.

I was hoping and gambling that the worm couldn't resist. And it didn't. Its front segments reared up, and the terrible mouth opened to show every shiny saw-tooth, ready to snap up the grisly titbit.

But as my severed finger dropped into that hungry mouth, I gripped the knife tightly and sprang upward, ignoring the pain as my damaged right hand clutched at the tendrils.

And my favoured left hand drove the golden blaze of the knife up into the monster's open mouth, and on up into its brain.

6

It probably wasn't a very big brain, but I didn't miss. The thing collapsed like a deflated balloon. I dropped down and stood watching its foul blood gush, watching it shrink and wither away to nothing as dying demon stalkers always did.

My wild half-idea had been right. Fray was a powerful sorcerer, but he was no mastermind. Armour of any kind is worn on the outside. It hadn't occurred to him to put magical shielding on the *inside* of his creature's mouth.

Then I turned quickly as April moaned. She was trying to sit up, though her left side was still paralysed. Fortunately, psychic healing was one of the powers included on her list and I watched as her eyes tightened in concentration. She seemed lost within herself for a moment as colour returned to her cheeks and she raised herself up to sitting.

'OK?' I asked.

'OK.' She smiled, getting slowly to her feet, fully recovered at last.

We both looked warily around, April using ESP as well – like a meerkat on alert for predators. But there was no sign of Fray or any other danger. And his magic had gone with him, for the fence and gate were back to the way we'd first seen them. My finger was mostly grown back too. Then I felt April's power swell around me like a musical chord I couldn't quite hear. The mud and blood vanished from our clothes, and the building materials flew back into their piles. Even the shattered wooden beam was neatly repaired.

'I hate leaving a mess,' she said happily.

As we got through the gate, back on to the street, we met a gang of workmen heading for the site with a JCB digger and one of those big long-armed power-drill machines. They paid us no attention, and we hurried past. Lucky they hadn't come along five minutes sooner, I thought.

Most ordinary people – magical types call them the Powerless – simply don't see magic even when it happens in front of them. It's too mind-crunchingly impossible, too far beyond belief and beyond their reality.

But it would have been hard for those men not to notice their fence changing back to normal, maybe even seeing the last of the monster withering away to nothing. And being forced to see such unbelievable things has been known to damage some people's minds.

As we moved away we both kept looking watchfully around. We knew that Fray would surely try again, sooner or later. But before that we were going to get into Paddy's house.

One of the things about the so-called 'higher' magic, I've learned, is that no matter how powerful a mage might be, his power doesn't work that well over distance. Which is a good thing, since otherwise the Cartel sorcerers could have just reached out magically, long ago, and erased me.

But distance isn't so much of a problem for the *psychic* powers. Definitely not for April's. She probably could have done a scan of Paddy's house from the far side of the city. But she was still getting used to the full range of her powers. After all, she'd only had control over them for a few weeks. So she wanted to look around the house with her eyes as well.

So did I, since I had nothing else to look with. The two of us together stood a better chance of finding some clue that would tell us where to look for Paddy and Julia – if any such clues existed. And I wanted to see for myself if there were any Cartel booby traps. And to watch for whatever warnings the knife might give.

It was late morning, people were at work or still in

bed, and the street where Paddy's house stood was silent and empty. We stopped a few houses away from Paddy's place, lurking behind a bushy shrub while April did her thing. She was checking everything about the house – doors and windows, walls and roof, the thin gravel on the front garden, even the asphalt path.

Then suddenly she stiffened with a gasp.

'Nick,' she whispered, 'there's someone *inside*!'

For a crazy hopeful moment I thought it might be Paddy, but of course April would have known that at once. She would have known if it was Fray too.

I reached for the knife. 'What kind of someone?'

'Some man,' she said. 'Someone I don't know.'

He might not be Cartel, I thought. Maybe not even magical. The knife's luminous glow was still silver. But that could just be because we were too far away.

'I'm going closer,' I murmured, and moved away as stealthily as anyone could along an open and deserted city street. April came with me, tense and frowning as her ESP went on studying the stranger in the house.

'Whoever it is, he's moving around,' she whispered. 'Into the front hall . . .'

By then we'd almost got to the gate, crouching down behind the thin hedge of the house next door. Not that trying to hide would do much good, I knew, if the man inside the house had the power to sense us the way April sensed him.

At the same time, though we were very close, I was relieved to see that the knife blade was still silvery. Whoever the stranger was, he definitely wasn't Cartel.

And then we both jumped as Paddy's front door flew open.

The man standing in the opening was stocky and broad-shouldered, wearing a short dark coat and baggy trousers. His thick hair was grey, his tangled beard was grey, his eyebrows looked like grey thickets. And beneath them, among deep lines and creases, his wintry-pale grey eyes gleamed at us.

'Mornin',' he rumbled, in a deep voice with some kind of vaguely rural accent. 'You'd best come in.'

7

We straightened up from our pointless crouches, but stayed where we were, ready to run or fight if we had to.

'Who're you?' I asked.

'And what are you doing in Paddy's house?' April added.

The man in the doorway hadn't moved. 'The name's Sam Foss. And you can put that knife away, lad. I'm not Cartel and not your enemy. I'm one of Paddy's oldest friends.'

So he was magical, since he could see the knife. But I didn't put it away, even though it was still placidly silver.

'I never heard him mention you,' I said.

'Paddy didn't talk much about other folk,' the man growled.

'You still haven't said what you're doing here,' April said.

His crooked half-smile was almost hidden in his

beard. 'Hopin' to find somethin' that'd tell me where Paddy and Julia went. And the last few days, waitin' for you two.' He took a half-step back. 'Now, are you comin' in, or do we talk out here where everyone can listen?'

April and I glanced at one another, then moved warily towards the door. And the man, Foss, turned away into the house, as if expecting us to follow.

He led us along the hallway, where I saw scorch marks on one wall left by the Cartel attack when they kidnapped April. The familiar lounge gave me a jolt of sadness, remembering happy times there with Paddy and Julia. Then I twitched again as Foss moved a magical hand and brought from nowhere a hovering yellow sphere that spread light and warmth around us.

'Sit yourselves down,' he said, settling himself in a chair.

'Mr Foss,' April said, 'have you thought that the Cartel might have left some sort of trap in here . . . ?'

'They did,' he growled. 'A couple of nasty little spy things. I got rid of them. And call me Sam. It's easier.' He offered his half-smile again. 'And you'll be Nick Walker, the Changeless Boy himself –' I saw him glance at the mark on my throat – 'and high-powered April, who doesn't know her full name because she has lost her memory.'

'Did Paddy tell you about us?' I asked, scowling.

'Thought you said he didn't talk about other people much?' April added.

Sam nodded, his smile fading. 'He told me – for a reason. He said there could be Cartel trouble brewin', and if anythin' happened to him and Julia he wanted me to look after you two.' His face twisted. 'And some-thin' *has* happened to them – I had a bad ESP sense of it, weeks ago. Along with a sense that you two were on your way here. So I've been waitin'.'

I was still scowling. 'We don't need *looking after*.'

'I know that,' he said. 'I get a sense that you faced serious trouble this mornin', and handled it. I don't mean to take *charge* of you. But Paddy wanted me to help you, so that's what I plan to do.'

April glanced at the hovering sphere of bright warmth. 'So you have psychic powers *and* the higher magic both?'

'Both.' He nodded. 'Don't you?'

April blinked, startled. 'No. Why would you think so?'

Sam shrugged. 'Paddy wondered. He said that even though your psychic powers broke out, you still had a heavy-duty barrier in your mind – and it seemed too much just to block your *memory* . . .' Seeing her frown, he hurried on. 'No matter. As for me, I'm a middlin' psychic – not on your level, lass, from what I hear. But

I have *plenty* of the higher magic. I'm the one who made that amulet Paddy wears.'

If that's true, I thought, he'd saved Paddy's life more than once. And he didn't seem to have the eyes of a liar. And April, who was nodding slowly, would have had some sense of any falseness in him . . .

So I stopped scowling, and we both relaxed, and he – Sam – seemed pleased.

'If you're ready to talk to me,' he said, 'you could start with what happened to you this mornin'.'

But as we started to tell him about the monster sent by Fray, he made us jump by lunging to his feet. 'A high-level Cartel sorcerer trackin' you?' he growled. 'You could've mentioned that sooner. We'd better get out of here.'

He headed for the hallway, and we followed. 'Where to?' I asked. 'Are we going by magic?' April asked.

Sam shook his head. 'I'll take you to my house, south of the river. Not by magic – a powerful mage could pick up its trail. And no standing at bus stops for us,' he laughed. 'We'll get a plain old ordinary anonymous taxi.'

8

We found one almost at once, so Sam must have worked *some* magic. Then he used the magic of money, seeming to have a lot of it. The promise of a big tip made the driver ignore speed limits and most other road safety rules, getting us to where we wanted to be so fast I wondered why his tyres hadn't melted.

Sam's two-storey house was solid, plain and very well kept, like all the houses in the fairly posh area where he lived. People around there had front gardens of tidy lawns and trim rose bushes, not stained mattresses and broken fridges as in Paddy's neighbourhood.

Inside, the house was warm and bright with thick carpets, comfortable furniture and colourful pictures on the walls. We perched on a sofa, peering around, as Sam sank into a cushiony armchair that was probably his favourite.

'That's better,' he said cheerfully. 'We've bought ourselves some time at least.' He smiled. 'Now I think we need a little treat, while you go on tellin' me about yourselves. And about Paddy and Julia.'

He moved a hand and a low table appeared in front of us, with a pot of hot coffee and a plateful of pastries. And we settled back and told him – talking with our mouths full some of the time – what he wanted to know.

His eyebrows drew down into a glower as he listened. He grunted with shock when we told what had been done to us at the Cartel house and looked appalled when we described Paddy's and Julia's disappearance. But he grinned fiercely when he heard how we'd got away, and how we'd fought the worm-monster that morning.

'A pair of real fighters, aren't you?' Sam said with a smile, though his eyes held a glint of respect.

'April's the fighter, with all her powers,' I said wryly. 'I'm just a survivor. I'd be long dead if it wasn't for her.'

Sam nodded. 'That may be so. Paddy told me about April's psychic power. But he told me about you, too, Nick. And I don't think you should talk as if you're just a *passenger*.'

'Definitely not,' April agreed.

'I heard about some of the demons you've faced,' Sam went on. 'Now you tell me you even killed that winter-demon, the Skryl . . . Nick, you've turned yourself into a *warrior*.'

I shook my head, embarrassed. 'I'm not. A bit hard to kill, maybe, because of being changeless. But mostly I've just been lucky.'

'Luck is a good thing, for a warrior,' Sam said. 'So is bein' hard to kill. But warriors need courage, and quick thinkin', and a total stubborn refusal to admit defeat. And you have all that too. Bags of it. You both have.' He peered at us intently. 'Whatever has to be done to find Paddy and Julia and get them back, I'll feel a lot better about doin' it with you two along. So, now – tell me again, every bit of it, how they disappeared.'

When he had made us repeat every detail of exactly what had happened, so that he was sure he'd got the complete picture, he sat back, looking thoughtful. 'It's good to know April had no sense of them dyin',' he growled. 'But I don't suppose Redman sent them to the seaside. Even though he didn't use a big spell or ritual, I think he might've sent them . . . Beyond.'

The way he said that last word chilled my spine. Manta had used it too, when she warned me about the Skryl . . .

'Beyond what?' April asked.

'Beyond this world, our *reality*,' Sam said. 'Where there are lots of other realms, other dimensions . . . Some are demon realms like the one your Skryl came from, Nick. But most of them are just weird Other Places.'

April looked as chilled as I felt. 'Do you have any idea which one Paddy and Julia might be in?'

Sam's half-nod became a shrug. 'There've been rumours, hints – about a special realm in the Beyond that the Cartel has taken over. It's said they keep a magic link to it permanently open, so it only takes a quick spell to send someone there. And the rumours say they use it as a place of *punishment*. Sort of their own private hell.'

I felt sick at the thought of Paddy and Julia being in such a place, and April's eyes glistened with tears. 'Can *you* get to that place?' I asked through gritted teeth.

He shrugged again. 'I've no idea what or where it is. But I'll do some serious sniffin' around, see what I can find out.' He scowled. 'If that's where our friends are, I'll find a way to it.'

'And take us with you,' April and I said at the same time.

He nodded slowly. 'I'll need all the help I can get. But let's not get ahead of ourselves. There's work to do just findin' out about it.'

'We need to move quickly,' April said pointedly. 'Paddy and Julia have been gone too long already.'

'I know,' Sam growled. 'I'll be quick as I can. But even if I can find out where the place is and how to get to it, that's just the first problem.' His eyes darkened.

'It could take a hell of a lot more work – and maybe more magical power than I have – to get all of us back *out* again.'

9

April and I felt pretty uneasy over the next few days. The Cartel's private hell – we couldn't guess at what such a place would be like, or how we could survive there. Or how we could help Paddy and Julia, if they were even there, let alone how or if we'd ever be able to make it back out again.

So many ifs, so many doubts, so many possible terrors . . . In the end we tried to make ourselves stop thinking about it. But we couldn't stop the nightmares.

Strangely, though, none of my dreams ever featured Manta.

After she first cast the spell that made me changeless, she had infested my dreams – usually telling me how I should learn to appreciate the great *gift* she'd given me. But she sometimes also gave me warnings – mostly, maddeningly, too vague – of dangers to come.

So it became clear that when I dreamed of Manta it wasn't really me dreaming. It was her, magically sending me dream-messages.

Then the Cartel tricked me, sending me a false dream of Manta, to lure me into their trap. And after that – since escaping from their clutches – I'd had no more dream-visions of her.

That could have meant that the Cartel had finally caught up with her. If they had, she was almost certainly dead.

Always, before, I'd felt mostly anger towards her, for making me what I am, *using* me, which had set the Cartel and their killers on my trail. But I'd come to see that she had no real choice. Above all, she'd been on the right side in the magical battle, a powerful enemy of the Cartel. So I'd never wished her dead. And now the thought of it saddened me.

Once, in fact, I hoped to find her and force her to lift the spell, make me normal again. Not that I had any idea how I could force a really dangerous witch to do anything. And anyway I was no longer sure that it could be done.

Fray had mockingly told me it was impossible. Reversing Manta's spell would mean *changing* me. And I couldn't be changed by anything this side of death.

Still, what Fray had said was only *logically* true. And magic often seems able to bypass logic. Besides, I knew that Fray would say anything if he knew that it might make someone suffer.

Besides, I'd been having second thoughts.

Even if I could be made normal again, so I could leave the country and escape the Cartel, I wasn't sure I'd want to. I'd not only be powerless, I'd also be totally *alone* again. Friendless.

I'd never had real friends before. Now that I had some – Paddy, Sam, especially April – I didn't want to lose them.

Especially when I'd be running away, leaving them to face the Cartel.

So I wasn't going to ask Sam about Manta's spell. Not then, when he was busy, and maybe not ever.

Anyway, I had more important questions for him, when there was time. Most of all about April.

She still remembered nothing about her past, except some vague memories of the first time she was the Cartel's prisoner, when she was little. But I'd come to believe that I knew something important about her.

Manta had told me when I first met her that she hated the Cartel because it had taken her 'most treasured possession'. And in a later dream-message, urging me to leave Paddy's so I wouldn't bring danger to the others, Manta also urged me to protect myself.

Because, she'd said passionately, 'they must not take *another child of mine*'.

That seemed to mean, weirdly, that she thought of me as hers. Because she'd made me what I am. But, more importantly, she'd said 'another' – the Cartel once *had* taken a child of hers. A very treasured possession . . .

So I became convinced that April was Manta's daughter.

Paddy had scoffed at the idea, and I'd never mentioned it to April. But I thought I might try the notion on Sam. And ask him too if he'd try to do what Paddy had tried – break the remaining blockage in April's mind and give her back her memory.

But I'd have to wait for a time when Sam wasn't spending all day, every day, poring over his huge store of ancient magical books and scrolls. Looking for some mention, some hint, of the dire realm that was the Cartel's private hell.

And getting nowhere.

'This is such a nice *quiet* area,' April said brightly. 'You never get a lot of people in the street or loud music or anything. You hardly even get cars going by. Totally *peaceful*, all the time.'

'Right,' I said with a wry smile. 'I'm bored silly too.'

She giggled. 'Sam said if we were all that bored we could always invite Fray round.'

'He'll probably come round anyway, before long,' I muttered. There was only so long we could hope to keep ourselves hidden from someone with Fray's powers.

April frowned. 'And if he has been kicked out, as he said in that dream of yours, the Cartel could be after us as well, *separately*.'

That unhappy thought had occurred to me too. Which was why staying in and being bored was probably better than fighting for our lives.

'When did you see Sam?' I asked, changing the subject.

'This morning, before you got up,' she said. 'Just for a few minutes. And we were talking about how psychics with PK can *reach out* for things when they need them. He told me that I should have a fairly long reach . . .'

She lifted one slim hand – and I jumped as a long shiny sword suddenly appeared in it.

'I never really tried it over distance before,' she said, smiling. 'But, Nick, I can reach just about any place in the city!' She waggled the sword. 'This is from the museum where you nearly died.'

I wasn't keen on revisiting that memory. 'Nice sword,' I said sourly. 'Nice *power*. I wish Manta had given me something like that instead.'

Her smile vanished, along with the sword, as she peered at me. 'She gave you a lot, Nick. And you've done a lot with it. Remember what Sam said.'

'Yeah, yeah,' I muttered. 'I'm a warrior. Me and Batman.' I waved a hand.

'Let's talk about something else. Or see what's on TV.'

And that was when Sam came in to tell us we were going out.

10

Sam had looked, he told us, through every scrap of magical writing he owned. And he'd been magically contacting other mages, along with trying what he called 'seeking' spells. And he'd found nothing, except the same vague hints – that a special dark realm had been turned into a prison by the Cartel, which could be where Paddy and Julia were.

So we were going to the library.

But Sam didn't mean one of the public libraries where I'd spent a lot of time – to keep warm as well as to read books – during my wanderings. He meant a place known only to high-level mages, where really ancient or secret or scary magical writings were kept, within all sorts of protections.

He hadn't wanted to go there if it wasn't necessary, because it cost a small fortune to get into that library. But Sam was sort of rich, from business deals. So he was willing to pay the price, as more or less a last resort.

'You two won't be allowed in the vault where the

scrolls and things are,' Sam told us. 'But the library's one of the safest places in the city, so you'll be all right while I'm readin'.'

I thought it sounded like more boredom. But it would be something just to get out of the house. So April and I grabbed a couple of ordinary books to read while we waited, and off we went.

Sam called another cab. It was a slower ride through the city this time, through the clogged pre-Christmas streets on a wet gloomy day. And, surprisingly, we ended up at an old bookshop that I knew fairly well, in the city centre near the big museum where April had got the sword.

The shop sold books about magic, folklore, fortune telling, all that. But the writings that Sam was looking for were in a secret cellar – which I'd never guessed at – below the shop's basement. Sam's magic opened an invisible door, bypassed the protections and got us in. And there we sat in a well-lit room, reading, yawning, sighing now and then, reminding ourselves that peace and quiet was lots better than being attacked by monsters.

But when Sam came out of the inner vault wearing a pleased and cheerful grin, we both sat up quickly. It looked like boredom might be coming to an end.

'I found somethin',' Sam announced. 'Some mystic in the west country who died years ago wrote a note about a place where evil sorcerers don't just send *people*, to punish them. They send people's *spirits* there too. Which might help.'

'How?' April asked.

'Tell you later,' Sam said. 'When I've looked into it. Let's get home.'

We left the shop in a hurry, looking for another cab, keen to get home so that Sam could finish his research and get us a step closer to finding Paddy and Julia.

On the ride home our mood stayed cheerful. Finally we were making some headway. And we were still chatting happily as we started up the path to Sam's front door.

Sam was absently digging out his keys, and April was smiling at something he'd said, so they didn't notice anything out of the ordinary. But as I trailed behind them after sorting out the fare with the cab driver, I felt a growing sense that something wasn't quite right.

I could have sworn that the flagstones of Sam's front path were a pale greyish-pink colour. But now those stones somehow seemed different, darker, much more red. Weirdly, they also seemed broader and thicker.

I blinked at them for an instant. Then as I started to say something to make the others look, I automatically half drew the knife and glanced at it.

The blade was a luminous gold.

I just had time to choke out a warning as all the big,

heavy red stones leaped up from the ground, tipping us into a tumbled heap on the lawn.

And then they gathered themselves into a terrifying shape, looming over us.

11

The stones seemed to be held together by invisible strings, vaguely in the form of a massive creature – huge-bodied and heavy-legged, with a shapeless head and a long thick tail.

I saw Sam move a hand, I saw the flicker of power in April's eyes, but the huge weird shape didn't move.

'Shielded,' Sam growled urgently.

'Like the worm-monster,' April said.

But then all the blocks of stone began to flow together, the spaces between them closing up and vanishing. In an instant they formed into one solid shape, like a statue badly carved from crimson stone, a crude image of an enormous four-legged beast like a dinosaur.

A *moving* statue – whose head was now more clearly formed, with glassy, glaring eyes and powerful jaws full of huge stony teeth.

As it took a lumbering step towards us, I saw Sam and April try their powers again. Still the monster wasn't harmed. And as we backed away, the massive body twisted and the heavy length of its tail whipped around with terrifying speed – smashing into Sam, hurling him like a missile to crash into April.

The two of them were flung to the ground some metres away. Where Sam lay still in a crumpled heap, with April moaning beside him.

And the monster thundered across the grass towards them, fanged jaws gaping.

I raced after it. I wasn't much for wrestling giant statues, and I knew the knife probably wouldn't be much use against the stony power of this monster. But I couldn't just stand and watch while it killed my friends.

The thing reared up, as if to bring both vast front feet crushingly down on April and Sam. I shouted, 'April! *Move!*' Then I leaped as high as I could towards the giant head.

The knife scraped across one glassy eye. It left only a small thin scratch, but that seemed to distract and delay the monster just enough. In its half-second hesitation, before the massive forefeet stamped down, April's PK shifted Sam and herself across the lawn and out of the way.

As I dropped back from the top of my leap, the monster crashed down to all fours, opening its terrible mouth as if to roar. But instead, staying eerily silent, it whirled with that same uncanny speed – and clamped its jaws on to my upper body, shook me like a terrier with a rat and threw me aside.

Half crushed and in agony, I hit the ground hard and lay sprawled and bleeding. I had several broken bones, and the stone fangs had done other internal damage. But they'd missed my heart. I was still alive, and I wouldn't be in pain for long.

Groaning, I made myself put a mental lid on the pain, while another bit of my mind fixed on an image – of the faint scratch made by the knife across the monster's eye. And with it came a thought, as bright as a searchlight.

The scratch meant that the shielding around the monster only protected it from *magical* attack. And just being stone would protect it from a blade. But maybe not from a machine.

'April!' I croaked. 'Can you get the power-drill machine from the site?'

She was recovering too, restoring herself. And as usual, she knew instantly what I meant.

With the stone monster lurching towards them, her incredible PK power reached out, halfway across the city, to the building site where we'd fought the giant worm.

But she didn't just *fetch* the big drilling machine. She brought it like a high-speed battering ram.

It crashed with enormous force into the monster's

huge stone body, flinging it to the ground in a shower of red stone chips mixed with splinters of the machine's metal. But the long drill-arm wasn't damaged by the impact.

As the stony horror started to get to its feet, the drill started up, powered by April's PK. The super-hard steel hammered at the monster's head in a blur of rapid-fire strikes like a big, noisy, metal woodpecker, spraying chunks of stone everywhere.

Even then the creature's tail lashed around, denting the side of the machine. But the drill-arm, undamaged, simply chopped the tail off and pounded it into gravel.

And so the drill kept on. Before the half-shattered monster could find its feet, it no longer had feet. Or legs. And the huge bulk of the body soon vanished as well, reduced to a small mountain of pulverized stone.

Which began to shrink and disappear, as defeated demon stalkers do, until only a tiny pinch of reddish powder was left to drift away on the breeze.

Though I wasn't fully restored by then, I managed to limp over to join April as she knelt beside the motionless body of Sam.

'He's alive,' she breathed, her voice trembling. 'But he's really hurt, Nick. And I don't think I know enough about the insides of bodies to fix all his injuries.'

I didn't know what to say or how to help. But I didn't

have to. Sam opened one eye, bleary and dulled with pain.

'Can fix . . . myself,' he croaked. 'Must . . . sleep.'

That cheered us both up. 'I'll get him inside,' April said. And her PK lifted him carefully and floated him along with her as she headed for the house.

At the door she paused. Her amazing power kept Sam hovering for a moment while it also repaired the drill machine and sent it back, tidied up the lawn and even restored my torn and blood-stained clothes.

Then she smiled. 'Nice one, by the way, thinking of the drill. That was *fun*.'

I was smiling too as she went in. But before I got myself through the door, a sharp posh voice behind me made me jump.

'Excuse me!' it said. 'What was all that noise? It sounded like *hammering*, and some kind of *machinery*!'

I turned to see Sam's next-door neighbour, a thin, bald, sniffy-looking man wearing a cardigan and staring at me suspiciously. I suppose in that area I looked like a fairly suspicious character.

'I think it was something going along the street,' I said vaguely.

He peered around, sniffing doubtfully, but saw no sign of noisy machinery. I could see he was dying to know who and what I was, but of course it wasn't polite

56

to ask. Instead he asked, 'Whatever happened to the path there?'

'Being replaced,' I said, putting a little sharpness in my voice to suggest that it wasn't any of his business.

He backed off at once, peered around with another sniff and went away. And another day it all might have made me laugh.

But right then I was too busy hoping we'd be able to manage so well when Fray tried for us again.

12

April was in Sam's kitchen, so I reckoned that she'd put Sam upstairs in his bedroom to get on with his healing sleep. I went up as well to wash and change my shirt, getting rid of a few specks of blood that April's repair work had missed.

I was completely back to normal by then, and I forced myself not to start fretting about another attack just yet. I'd found that Cartel attacks hardly ever came at non-stop, one-after-another speed. There was always a lull, while they thought of what to try next or recharged their sorcery batteries or whatever.

So, just then, we had a while when we could put dark and fearful thoughts aside. Standing at the window of my room, I wasn't scanning for enemies but watching the winter sunset and relishing the quiet, broken only by a few sleepy birds.

I'd never lived in such a nice place, I thought wistfully. Definitely not when I was a neglected little kid with my mum or a lonely hungry bigger kid on the streets. I could hardly imagine what it would be like to own a home like Sam's, and live there without worrying about where my next meal – or next monster – would come from. Looking out at the smooth grass and bright-leaved bushes in the back garden, I imagined myself sitting out there on a summer evening, enjoying the air, having a quiet drink with April . . .

I shook myself. In your dreams, I told myself. Not in this life.

Sam stayed silent in his room all through the evening. April checked on him regularly, but he seemed to be just sleeping. And with a bit of tension growing in us as we waited for him to surface, along with some reaction from the fight with the stone monster, we both went up to our rooms fairly early.

But the peace and quiet didn't go with us.

We decided to look in on Sam, to be sure he was all right. But what we saw told us little and wound up our tension another few notches.

The lights were off in Sam's room, but there was a large pale-blue sphere, glowing softly, hovering above the bed. And Sam was inside the sphere, floating, motionless, his eyes closed. He was entirely wrapped in gauzy silvery cloth, looking like an oversized cocoon, but with stray bits of grey hair and beard poking out to prove it was him. So we stared, and blinked, and crept away.

'That was amazing,' April said. 'I wish I knew more about the higher magic.'

'I'm just glad Sam does,' I muttered.

After that, I had some extra-scary nightmares. None of them featured Manta or Fray or anyone I knew, just a series of horror images. Including one where the whole house started shaking and groaning like a giant beast, until the roof was ripped open and an enormous, clawed, hairy hand came reaching in from the darkness towards me.

And when in the dream the hand took hold of me, it was just as well I was so deeply asleep that I fumbled my frantic grab at the knife under my pillow.

Because I really *was* being clutched. By April, in her pyjamas, wide-eyed and frightened, shaking me awake.

'Nick!' she breathed. '*Listen!*'

I sat up, instantly awake and rigid with shock.

Beyond the door of my room, the house seemed to be filled with the sound of many hollow echoing voices, moaning and wailing.

It was as creepy as any of my bad dreams. And I realized that it was coming from Sam's room, down the hall. I leaped out of bed, snatching up the knife. But its blade was an untroubled silver.

'I can't sense anyone or anything in there except

Sam,' April whispered. 'But it *sounds* like a mass of people!'

'More weird magic,' I muttered, as we crept nervously down the hall.

At Sam's door the knife was still silver and April's ESP still sensed no danger. But when we slowly, nervously, pushed the door open we barely managed to keep ourselves from crying out with fright.

In Sam's room all the furniture – the bed, a table, a wardrobe, a rug – had been pushed back against the walls. The walls themselves seemed to be glowing faintly, pale-blue like the sphere that we'd seen Sam floating in before.

But now he stood in the middle of the empty space, with the gauzy silver cloth around him like a flowing robe. And he was standing inside a strange pattern that had been drawn or painted on the polished boards of the floor, its lines glimmering bright blue, while in the area between that pattern and the glowing blue walls, shadows were floating and swirling. Shapeless shadows, which were making the weird moaning sounds.

'Nick,' April whispered, 'those moving things . . . They aren't just shadows.'

I stared at the drifting shapes, feeling the hairs on my neck lift. Looking closely, I could see the hollow-eyed twisted human faces, the wide-gaping mouths.

I glanced down again, seeing with relief that the

knife was still silver. Then April and I flinched as some of the ghostly shadows began to swirl towards us, long, thin, hazy arms reaching out.

Sam swung around to stare at us, his eyes dark, his craggy face looking tense and strained. And his voice seemed deeper than ever, booming as if from some unknown cavernous depths.

'*Begone!*' he roared.

And we fled in a wild scramble like terrified children.

13

'I thought at first that it was another attack,' April gasped.

'The knife said not,' I said, hearing a tremor in my own voice. 'And it didn't look like he was in trouble.'

'No,' she agreed. 'It had to be some kind of ritual. He seemed to be *controlling* those shadow-things . . .'

'I suppose he'll tell us, come morning,' I said.

We were at the kitchen table, shakily sipping tea, with our backs to the windows. Outside, it was probably just an ordinary quiet dark night in the suburbs. But we didn't want to look, in case those shadows were moving too . . .

And we also tried not to wonder what was happening upstairs, where the eerie sounds had stopped.

'I just hope we didn't break some important magical law or something, going in there,' April murmured.

'Don't fret,' Sam's voice said, behind us. 'Openin' the door broke the enclosure for a moment. But no harm done.'

We turned. Sam was fully dressed and upright and looking like himself again, with no sign of any effects from the stone monster's attack or the ritual in his room. Except for a trace of weariness deepening the lines around his eyes.

'Anyway, it worked,' he growled. 'I've learned more about that place – the realm that's a private Cartel hell. And more or less *where* it is. I'm even fairly sure that Paddy and Julia are there.' His face twisted. 'Trouble is, I still have no earthly idea how to get there.'

April went white, and maybe I did too as we just stared at him, stunned.

He sat down at the table, sighing. 'What you saw was a special ritual, not easy to do and fairly dangerous. It put me in touch with a group of powerful shamans from ancient times, pre-civilization.'

'You mean their ghosts?' April asked.

'Not exactly,' Sam said. 'More like their . . . essences. They don't have bodies now, but they still have most of their powers, which ghosts don't. And they know a lot – especially about the Beyond, and what could be called the *spirit realms*. So they know about the Cartel's hell-place, because the Cartel sends spirits there as well as live people.' He smiled grimly. 'The ancients aren't too friendly to anyone. But they *really* don't like the Cartel. Some of its sorcerers tried to enslave them once.'

'But they didn't tell you how to get to the Cartel place,' I said.

'No. It seems there's a special Cartel magic needed to get there or send people there. And it's very secret and extra protected, so even the ancient ones can't find it.' Sam grimaced. 'They told me to forget about tryin' to go there. They called it a place of *evil mist and torment* – and they said I really wouldn't like it.'

'What about Paddy and Julia?' April asked.

'I don't know for sure,' Sam said. 'The ancient ones reached out to the place, for me, and sensed two new presences there, live ones, a man and a woman. But that's all they could tell me.'

'Are they suffering there, if it's them?' April whispered.

Sam looked grim. 'They won't be enjoyin' it. The place is all gloomy emptiness and weird mists. And anyone sent there *alive* has to keep walkin' along some kind of magical road. The ancient ones called it the Downward Path.'

'Where does it lead to?' I asked.

'No idea,' Sam growled. 'Anyway, the point is that for us to get to that place, on to the Downward Path, we'd need to know the special magic spell that Cartel sorcerers use to send people there.'

'So it's hopeless,' I muttered.

'Maybe not,' Sam said, surprising us. 'I had the idea

that we might just go and catch a Cartel sorcerer, and do whatever we have to do to make him *tell* us.' His grin was fierce and humourless. 'So let's get Fray.'

It was amazing how that notion cheered us up. Sam had a dozen ideas for different kinds of magical traps that might imprison Fray and stop him using his power. And I had a really good time thinking up ways to get my own back and make Fray talk.

But April looked doubtful. 'It won't be that easy,' she said. 'We don't have any idea where Fray is.'

'Not a problem,' Sam said, waving a hand. 'He knows where *we* are. So I'll set up a little backtrackin' spell – and we'll stay watchful and ready, and wait for the next monster or whatever. Then, after we deal with it, my spell should be able to follow its magical trail back to Fray.'

Magical backtracking sounded amazing, but as usual Sam seemed to know what he was talking about. And the first step of the plan was easy enough, though it didn't sound like fun.

We just had to sit tight, stay alert and wait. Fray seemed to want to send monsters to kill us, so we'd have to be ready for another.

But he surprised us.

14

Through the next long day or two – and the even longer night or two, when we didn't sleep much – absolutely nothing happened except that our nerves got wound up fairly tight. But I hadn't expected anything that soon. We were still in the usual lull that happened between Cartel attacks.

Even so, April wasn't quite able to believe it. 'What do we do if he *doesn't* attack again? If he's given up, or been called off by the Cartel . . .'

'Not likely,' Sam said. 'People lookin' for revenge don't usually give up easily. And he told Nick clearly enough in that dream that he's been *excluded* – so he'll be on his own now, not on Cartel orders.'

'He must be,' I said. 'These last two monsters he sent were trying to *kill* us, both of us – and the Cartel always wanted to take April alive.'

'Maybe they changed their minds,' April said.

'I doubt it,' Sam said. 'I think Nick has got it right – Fray's insane. He was probably already well on the way – no one likes cruelty that much without bein' some way round the bend. And now he's so full of hate, wantin' revenge on you two so much, he's gone over the edge. Out of his mind and out of control.'

'Great,' I said. 'A magical maniac.'

'It sounds like bad news,' Sam said, 'but maybe it isn't. When you're doin' magic you need to be in control. Or else you go wrong, make mistakes. Which is what Fray's been doin'. Think about it. He tries to scare you in that dream, Nick, but it just puts you on guard. He sends two big killer-monsters, but he doesn't get their shieldin' right. Most of all, he doesn't *learn*, so he keeps thinkin' you're easy targets.'

'He's still really powerful and dangerous,' April said.

'Yeah, well, so am I,' Sam said, smiling. 'And I'm not crazy. But Fray is – and he's probably worse now, havin' failed twice.'

'Three strikes and out,' I muttered.

After all that we relaxed a little – still watchfully on guard, but not wound up quite so twitchily tight. And as the lull continued for another day or two the three of us had some good times together. April and I encouraged Sam to tell some of his large fund of stories from his footloose earlier life as a mage – and April and I put in a few tales of our own, from our younger days of living rough before we'd met.

We also went out now and then, for some air and

68

exercise. Sam tried to interest April and me in what he called the joys of gardening, but I tried to make him see that *joy* and *gardening* couldn't happen at the same time. So we mostly just went for walks, staying away from crowds.

Until one morning, after we'd put on our coats to go out again, when we noticed three small puddles appear on the kitchen table, bright with rainbow colours.

We exchanged nervous glances as I drew back from the table, reaching for the knife to check its colour but, in the next fraction of a second, before April and Sam could move, the three bright little pools swelled into huge bubbles, and burst.

The soft explosions flung out broad rippling sheets of transparent filminess, thin and oily and sticky. Two of the sheets wrapped around April and Sam before they could move or speak – dragging them down to the floor, magically smothering their powers as well as their voices and movement.

But I'd already been moving away from the table, so I had time to slash at the third bubble with the golden knife. It collapsed – but I didn't get to move again.

A heavy javelin appeared from nowhere, flying at furious speed. As I tried to dodge, its wicked point punched into my chest and slammed me back against the wall, nailing me there like a pinned butterfly.

Stunned, agonized, bleeding, I dimly saw the door

crash open. And Fray stalked in, smiling his evil, glee-ful smile.

Once again he looked as I'd first seen him – bone-thin, stiff, in an elegant dark suit, his thick hair pure white, though he wasn't old. But as on the street by the building site, the metal braces held his ruined legs together and the shiny metal crutches held him upright. And his eyes were blazing, bulging, maniacal.

'Didn't expect *that*, did you?' he said with a weird giggle, grinning at me, then peering down at Sam and April. They lay unmoving, eyes closed, and sudden fear that they were dying brought me back to full awareness despite the shrieking pain of the javelin in my chest.

Fray prodded Sam with a crutch. 'I *know* you,' he muttered. 'Foss or something, isn't it? One of the so-called *independents* who think the Cartel doesn't notice them?' He laughed again, high and crazed. 'But I expect you'll tell me all about yourself. You'll tell me many things, when I introduce you to levels of pain that you cannot begin to imagine.'

As he giggled again, an agonized cough rose up within me. He spun around, in time to see me choke on a mouthful of bright blood. At once I slumped, closing my eyes, ignoring the agony as I hung there on the javelin.

'Ah,' Fray smiled. 'The Changeless Boy being changed at last, as death comes to embrace him.'

70

He turned away, back to April and Sam, still motionlessly wrapped in the sticky filminess. So he didn't see my eyes open a little, watching him through slits.

The javelin was murderously painful, but it had only grazed a lung. And while an ordinary person might have slowly drowned in their own blood, I wouldn't. I'd be restored before that happened, my internal injuries fixing themselves around the javelin's unforgiving form.

So Fray was making more mistakes. He believed that I was near death, no longer a threat. And when he'd turned for that moment to gloat over me, he'd failed to keep an eye on his two *magical* prisoners. He hadn't seen the tiny flicker of April's eyelids, the small movements of Sam's right hand.

Fray's evil magic wasn't as powerful as he thought. Sam and April were *fighting* the stuff that bound them.

So I had to do something to keep Fray from discovering that too soon and putting some other spell on them.

I gave a low, hollow groan, which wasn't entirely faked. Fray turned back with a grin to look at me again. To enjoy my pain, as I'd hoped. To watch me die.

April's eyes flickered again, and I saw her using her powers to peel the filmy stuff away from her face. Just as Sam's right hand clawed through the film holding him.

And I yelled with mingled pain and rage and jerked the javelin out of the wall and out of my chest.

Then I flung it at Fray – clumsily, right-handed – and lurched after it towards him, the knife glowing in my other hand.

Fray dodged the javelin, looking shocked, and began to raise a hand to flatten me with magic. Just as Sam and April both struck at him with *their* power.

That flung him, shrieking, halfway across the room. As I whirled towards him, Sam lunged to his feet, his face dark with fury, the filminess gone from around him. With April leaping up beside him, also free, her eyes flaring.

Fray had lost his crutches as he fell and lay thrashing on the floor, flecks of foam on his lips, eyes crazy-wild, holding up his hands in front of him as if in surrender, screaming in a high thin whine.

Seeing him like that, Sam and April hesitated. And Fray's screaming became shrill laughter.

'Do you seek to *defeat* me, fools? You will not *touch* me!'

Before Sam and April could strike again, he spat a harsh phrase while rapidly moving his hands. In a pattern that somehow looked familiar . . .

Suddenly the three of us were flying through the air at dizzying speed towards the kitchen wall. And before Sam or April could do anything, they ran out of time.

We didn't hit the wall. It and the house and Fray all vanished, into a darkness so deep and total that I could almost feel its weight.

I flew on through the darkness, not able to see Sam or April or anything else, not able to hear a thing – not even my own screaming.

Then at once the darkness gave way to cold, dim, grey light, like daybreak on a November morning. It seemed to seep through a thin mist gathering around me as I hurtled on.

In the next instant that terrifying flight came to an end, as I landed – on my feet, with hardly any jolt at all.

I was standing on a wide, flat, empty roadway. And I was utterly alone.

15

I don't remember much of what happened next. I think I went out of my mind. I know that I screamed and howled a lot – desperately, frantically shrieking Sam's and April's names, or just shrieking wordlessly in panic and despair.

I must have flung myself down on to the roadway too, or maybe I just fell over in the midst of that agonized madness. At the same time I was crazily lashing out with the knife at imaginary shadows, or at nothing much at all.

So when the survivor bit of me started to drag me back to sanity and awareness, I still had the knife in my hand, intact and luminous. Proving at last – as I'd always thought, but never tested – that the blade really was magically unbreakable.

All around me on the roadway where I'd been rolling and thrashing, I saw deep gashes in the hard rough surface. And my fists and feet hadn't made them.

By then my chest injury had healed and I was back

to normal. And I twitched a bit when I saw that the road was also changeless in its own way. All the gouges that the knife had made were slowly filling in and fading, so that in minutes the surface was just as it had been.

I saw all that in the knife's glow, an island of light in that place of gloom and greyness. The brightness, and the reassuring feel of the hilt in my hand, had also helped me back to something like sanity. Or anyway back on to my feet.

But the knife's glow was *golden*. Which might have meant that some Cartel horror was lurking nearby. But I knew, as I stared around, that more probably it was because the whole eerie, impossible place *belonged* to the Cartel.

Where I stood, the roadway sloped down – not very steeply – in one direction and sloped up in the other, for as far as I could see. On one side of the road, pale drifts of mist floated slowly like heavy curtains. Now and then they gave glimpses of bare stony ground, looking rougher than the roadway.

On the other side there was nothing to see. Literally. Just a total darkness that the knife's glow couldn't penetrate. Standing at the road's edge, I stretched out my left hand as far as I could, but the knife met only blank silent emptiness as dark as the spaces between stars.

The roadway offered no pebbles, so I took a small coin from my pocket and threw it into the darkness. In the knife's glow I saw it starting to fall, but the darkness swallowed it. And I realized that it must be some kind of bottomless void, because I never heard any sound of the coin landing.

An endless shadowy depth, spooky drifting mists, an empty magical roadway sloping down . . . I remembered Sam telling April and me what the ancient ones had called the private hell-realm made by the Cartel.

A place of 'evil mist and torment'. Where any *living* person sent there was doomed to walk endlessly along a way known as the Downward Path.

I knew that I was standing on it.

So Fray had done what Redman probably did to Paddy and Julia. He had sent me to the Cartel hell. With no chance of ever getting out.

That last thought nearly flung me back into another screaming collapse.

But a further thought kept me from it. If I was on that dire Path, I was in the place where Paddy and Julia might be.

And since Fray's spell had sent us all flying at the same time, Sam and April were probably there too. On some other bit, or bits, of the Path.

So the only four people that I'd ever really cared about could be somewhere along that eerie roadway.

Right, I told myself fiercely. Pull yourself together and go and find them.

I had no idea how to do that, but I refused to worry about it. I'd just arrived. I'd learn about the Path as I went along, and I'd find a way.

And if – no, *when* – I found the others, there had to be a chance that Sam's magic, maybe helped by April and Paddy, could find a way out.

So I tucked that hope away in my mind and started walking.

Only to find that I'd already *begun* walking, without realizing it. As if some outside force had got my feet into motion.

Frowning, I stopped, staring down at the Path. But there was nothing to see except the grey, slightly rough surface. A magical surface though, and not only because it couldn't be marked.

As I stared down, I felt a nagging inner urge, not hugely powerful but compelling enough.

And my legs and feet, as if by themselves, quietly and without fuss, started walking again.

So living people sent on to the Path had to keep walking. I wondered what they – we – did when we got tired or hungry or needed the toilet. But I expected I'd find out, in time. Meanwhile I walked on, because I had to.

It could have been worse, I thought. It wasn't warm on the Path, but it wasn't exactly cold either. And I was wearing my jacket. I'd survived much colder weather in lighter clothes.

So if I felt a little shivery, it came from being surrounded by the creepy evil magic of deadly enemies. But I'd survived that before, too.

At least the downward slope was easy enough to walk on, and I saw no obstacles of any sort ahead. Warily I paused and turned, but also saw nothing at all along the upward slope.

The Path's power started me walking again, in that direction, back the way I'd come. I gasped in surprise – somehow I was walking on a *downward* slope again.

Two more tries in either direction proved it. The Downward Path was called that simply because it went down, *whichever* way you walked.

I wondered whether the Path just kept on downward forever, or led to some kind of end, at the bottom of the slope. But I stopped that thought.

I was in a Cartel hell-place. I didn't want to think about – or find out – what might be waiting at the end of the Path.

Still, what I wanted didn't matter. I was walking the Path because its magic kept me going – but also, I thought, because I *needed* to keep going. I wouldn't find my friends by standing still, even if the Path would let me.

So I walked on, with an easy relaxed stride that I could keep up for a long time without getting tired. And I kept a careful watch on the Path ahead, and what I could see of it when I glanced back.

Ignoring the empty darkness on one side, I also kept peering intently into the mists on the other – hoping that some brief parting of the pale cloudiness would show me something more useful than blank stony ground.

And I tried to keep myself from getting down-hearted and desperate when nothing different at all showed up anywhere on that bleak, lifeless landscape.

Not until the shocking moment when something that was both man and beast slouched out of the mists on to the Path, baring huge fangs, to bar my way.

16

Some of my shock came from the fact that I'd met that monster before. On the long-ago night when Manta made me changeless.

Harne. The demon stalker who'd been sent to kill Manta. Until she put me in his way – and I got lucky with the knife I'd just been given and cut his throat.

So this would have to be the ghost of Harne, somehow come to the eerie gloom of the Path to haunt me.

Although, I thought, with the way he was showing his fangs and flexing his claws, maybe the Path had somehow brought him back to life and he'd come to kill me instead.

I raised the knife, shivering again as his presence turned the air colder. Just like home, I thought bitterly. Still being hunted by Cartel killers. Only now it's *dead* ones.

Maybe this is more of the evil magic of this place, I thought. To torment me as I walk, or to prevent me from finding the others.

Or maybe the Path likes the taste of blood.

'Your knife cannot harm me,' Harne growled, his voice weirdly hollow. 'Nothing you can do can harm me now. But we can harm you – and not even your changelessness will protect you.'

Out of all that vague chilling menace, one word leaped out. '*We?*' I said, looking behind me, seeing the Path as empty as before.

'Those who know you have sensed your arrival,' Harne snarled. 'All those you have killed are here. Because you still live, we are punished and must suffer in the mists beyond the Path. As you will soon suffer.'

As I shivered and listened, I suddenly realized that I could just make out a dim hint of the Path *behind* him. Harne's hairy bulk wasn't solid, but semi-transparent.

'I'm going to suffer?' I said through my teeth. 'You're a ghost, without a body. What are you going to do – scare me to death?'

Harne growled with rage. 'Though we are ghosts, you are not safe from us. Just as the girl-child, your friend, is not safe.'

That stabbed at every nerve-end in my body. '*April?* Where is she?'

The beast-man's grin was as horrible as his growl. 'She is in the mists, boy. With ghosts who hate her as I hate you. If you were brave enough to enter the mists, you would hear her screams.'

81

Something like a scream burst from my own lips as I leaped at him, knife flashing.

'*Tell me where she is!*'

Harne stepped back, but he was still grinning. The knife could no more harm him than it could cut the air. 'Come and seek her,' he growled. 'Come into the mists, if you dare.' His laugh was a monster's roar. 'But know that if you die in this realm, you will be here with us *forever*!'

Still in a fury, I swung the knife at him again. Laughing, unharmed, he drifted away, back towards the bank of mist that he had come from, fading and disappearing into it.

I didn't stop to worry about his threats. Demon stalkers always liked to tell me that I was going to die. But if April really was in the mists, in danger . . .

I followed the sound of Harne's cruel beast-laughter and plunged in after him.

It was mostly thin mist rather than dense fog, endlessly coiling and swirling and giving more brief glimpses of the stony ground. But not just the ground.

Though Harne had vanished, I still wasn't alone.

I could hear thin, high-pitched cries everywhere around me in the mist – blood-freezing cries, lost, desolate howling and wailing that lifted all the hairs on my back. None of them sounded like April. All of them sounded like ghosts.

And then the filmy shapes began lunging out at me from those haunted mists.

Familiar shapes, as Harne had been. An onrushing crowd of all the Cartel demons that I'd killed over the years, their cries filled now with hatred and evil glee.

First to appear was the lizard-boy Chlar with his poisoned scorpion tail – stabbing at me as he screamed in my face.

By reflex I flung myself aside, though I knew the vicious spike had no substance and couldn't hurt me. Howling, Chlar's ghost swooped away, replaced by more. The terrible Conrad, who could divide himself into six lethal warriors with blades for hands. Others from years before – the demonic knight in blood-red armour with his flaming lance, the four-armed giant with his spiked clubs, and more, and more . . .

None of their wraith-bodies could touch me, but their furious cries clawed at my mind while the bitter cold they brought seeped into my bones. And the instinctive human terror of the undead kept me flinching and dodging, adding my own horror-cries to theirs.

But I was also screaming April's name, still stumbling on through the mists in a frantic, despairing search. I had no clear idea of where I was or how to get back to the Path, and I didn't care. I wasn't going to stop searching as long as I was in one piece and on my feet.

In the next instant, as I plunged into a thicker bank of mist, something like a length of rubbery cord wrapped around my ankle and tightened.

Tumbling forward with a yell, I sprawled into a tangle of more cords, thick and flexible and as sticky as glue. Twisting, writhing, clinging, they wrapped around every bit of me and held me fast.

17

The ghosts fell silent, no longer whirling around me but drifting, watching my struggles – no doubt hoping to watch me die. And I quickly found that fighting the grip of the gluey, elastic cords only seemed to get me more tangled. But I kept fighting, unable to quell the desperate urge to escape.

The whole tangle was like a huge, shapeless, horizontal spider-web, spread to trap anything that came along. And I badly didn't want to meet the thing that made it.

But I was still stuck fast when I learned that it wasn't a thing. It was two things.

They looked like broad sheets of rumpled canvas, thick, ragged, dirty-white. With round bulges at the front showing small jutting eyes and mouths like viciously sharp beaks. They moved by flopping along the ground, and even though the cords didn't stick to their surfaces they weren't quick.

By then I'd got some sense back and stopped

struggling. Instead I concentrated on dragging my left hand free. My knife hand. And before the grisly beak of the first thing could take a bite out of me, I'd got enough movement in that hand to use the knife on whatever cords it could reach.

The cords didn't stick to the glowing blade. As they fell away I got my whole arm free and chopped wildly at the other cords holding me. And in the next movement I slashed furiously at the floppy body of the nearest creature.

The blade nearly cut the thing in half. Its flesh was as soft as rotting blubber, its blood was yellowish-thick like pus, and it all stank unbelievably. The stink got worse when I dodged the beak of the second one and chopped at it as well. As the two horrors thrashed and stank and died, I cut away the last cords to free the rest of me and scrambled away into the mists.

Before long I'd left most of the smell behind. But the ghosts were there again, screaming in a bedlam of hate and fury all around me – the ghastly chill clutching at my flesh, the unholy horror scraping at my mind.

As I stumbled on, I realized that Harne might have lied about April just to lure me into that nest of monsters. I definitely hadn't heard her screaming – though the cries of the ghosts might have drowned her out.

So I still had no idea which way to go. All I could do was keep blundering along and hope to get lucky.

'Lucky'. Definitely the wrong word for that place. People doomed to the hell of the Downward Path didn't bring luck with them. Nor hope either, I thought. Especially not in the soul-destroying desolation and horror of the haunted mists . . .

I came to a sudden stop, with a choked snarl. This is what they *want*, I told myself angrily. The ghosts and the place itself are going all out to take away your hope, weaken your mind, crush your will, until you give up and let yourself die.

Bring it on, I yelled silently, while the wraiths howled and the mists swirled. You won't stop me so easily . . .

In that moment I heard a faint sound like rattling pebbles behind me.

And I whirled to find that I was being followed by monsters.

They weren't much bigger than me, but that was the only good news. There were four of them, looking like plucked birds. They had the glaring evil eyes and long hooked beaks of vultures, scrawny necks, stringy but muscly bodies with dull grey skin. They had no wings, just skinny arms with claws for hands, and their bony legs ended in talons.

I saw all that in a second's glance, which was how

long it took them to size me up. Then they leaped at me with harsh cawing noises, beaks and claws reaching.

I slid to one side as they leaped, so only two of them landed on me, the three of us tumbling to the ground. One of those two got skewered by the knife as we fell, but the other fastened its beak on my arm and its claws in my shoulder. Yelling in pain, I tore myself partly out of its grip, sliced through its pencil-neck and rolled away.

The other two attacked from each side as I got to my feet. I steeled myself against more pain and turned my back on one, letting it sink its claws into my back, its vicious beak snapping at my neck. Facing the other, I blocked its lunge with the knife, which sheared through the beak. The thing fell back screeching until I drove the knife into one mad eye.

As its corpse dropped, so did I – throwing myself back and down with the fourth monster between me and the hard ground. I heard a bone snap, and as it shrieked I ripped my flesh away from its talons, spun and plunged the knife into its chest.

Unlike the demons sent to attack me in the real world which, in death, vanished into nothingness, these creatures lay, seeping out life, where they fell. I guess in the real world, the Cartel cleaned up after itself – it simply wouldn't do to have a load of decomposing demon corpses lying around!

Having checked the hideous vultures really were finished, I clambered slowly to my feet, awash with my own blood and theirs, and staggered away into the mists.

It was clear that that hell-place offered a lot of options for torment, despair and death. Anyone brave enough to venture off the Path into the mists, and mentally strong enough to resist the horror of the ghosts, would then face a dire assortment of creatures eager to eat them alive.

I didn't let myself worry about whether there might be more. I had a feeling I'd find out soon enough. And the howls of the ghosts, sounding even more maddened, seemed to agree.

Still, I realized, Fray in his craziness had been a bit hasty. He'd sent me to suffer on the Path – but I'd arrived intact, with my changelessness, an ability to withstand pain and a lot of experience of fighting demons. And with the knife.

So, I told myself, I had exactly what I'd had for years. The equipment that let me do what I do best. Survive.

Easy to say, maybe, but the thought got me going again, as my wounds closed and faded and I returned to normal.

Just in time to see, through a momentary gap in the mist, what was sliding around a boulder only a few steps ahead of me.

*

89

Another nightmare creature, looking like an overgrown beetle the size of a small car. It had a lot of many-jointed legs and two spindly antennae waving around above its bulging eyes. Its humped body was armoured in a thick, shiny black shell, except for a dark hairy patch on its underbelly. And every bit of it was also covered in needle-sharp spikes.

Not prickles or thorns or spines. *Spikes*. Shiny black like the rest of it, stiff and sturdy-looking and really long. With shorter spikes, just as sharp, on the legs. Its mouth was an insect's sharp pincer-jaws, and even its long black flickering tongue had short ugly barbed spikes.

I took several fast steps back. That was a lot of weaponry – and one of the longer spikes driven into my heart or brain would kill me instantly.

The relentlessness of the onslaught was beginning to get to me. Back in the real world I usually had days, at least, to recover between attacks. But not here. Bang, bang, bang, one monster after another came at me through the mists. For a moment I stumbled at the thought: what if the onslaught didn't stop? I faltered as the monster made a sudden scuttling rush, and its long spiky tongue flashed out at me.

I flung up my left arm, trying to block it with the knife, but missed. The tongue hit hard, making me stagger forward while its barbed spikes shredded my arm. The knife fell from what was left of my hand – and I fell too, yelling in agony, trying to dodge as the tongue struck again, ripping flesh from my right leg.

With the pain and shock, I could do little more than wriggle away along the ground, slowly and weakly. With the horror-bug scuttling after me, jaws clashing.

But it *was* a bug, mindless, driven by hunger. And I'd left a pool of my blood where I'd first fallen, not far behind me. So it stopped its charge, stuck out its grisly tongue again and began to lap.

And I turned, slithered back through more of my blood, scooped up the knife in my right hand and jammed it up into the thing's hairy underbelly.

The monster hissed like a deflating balloon, flailing at me with its spiky legs. But I was too close, almost underneath it, and most of the blows missed. And I hardly felt the ones that hit, for the creature was weakening and dying, and I was drifting into pain-free darkness.

It was one of those times when I felt surprised – as well as relieved – to be alive when I came back to myself. Somehow all the spikes had missed my vital bits. I wasn't another howling ghost trapped forever in the mists.

I was a total mess, as usual – my clothes torn and drenched with my own drying blood. But at least all my ravaged flesh was back to normal, free from pain.

Except for a small discomfort from the knife's hilt, underneath me where I lay.

I thanked my lucky stars that no other creature had crawled out to snack on me as I lay there unconscious. Then relief turned to jolting shock – as a voice spoke from somewhere above me.

'My word, young man,' the voice said, in a slightly mocking drawl. 'You *have* been through the wars.'

18

When I looked up, I thought I was seeing another ghost. The figure standing over me was wearing a long dark cloak with a deep hood shadowing the face and wide sleeves covering the hands. With swirls of mist floating around it, the effect was definitely spooky.

But then the hood pulled back a bit, as if by itself, to show the cloaked person's human face – male, in his thirties or early forties. Not bad-looking, with wavy brown hair, a firm jaw and clear hazel eyes.

He didn't look all that threatening, though he seemed out of place there, smiling calmly as if we'd met on a quiet city street rather than in a haunted mist. Still, as I got to my feet, I was on my guard. The knife didn't tell me anything, since it would always be golden in that Cartel realm. But for me, just then, everything was evil and dangerous until proved otherwise. So I watched him carefully, knife in hand.

'I do like that unusual knife,' he said, lifting an

eyebrow. 'Marvellous bit of colour in this bleak place. But whatever are you doing in the mists?'

His voice sounded trained, like some DJs or TV presenters. And he seemed to pose in that showy cloak and hood, which was too much like the costume of the standard comic-book wizard. I felt a *falseness* about him, an air of pretence that rang my alarm bells.

But he was still smiling, keeping his distance, so I replied. 'I came in looking for someone – a girl,' I said, keeping my face blank and my voice flat. 'The ghost of . . . someone I knew . . . told me that other ghosts had brought her in here. Maybe hurting her.'

'Oh, dear, no.' He shook his head sadly. 'That was a cruel lie. The ghosts can't *touch* anyone, let alone keep them against their will or harm them.'

So Harne's ghost *had* lied – to lure me in, I thought.

'Even the ghosts of mages lose their power here,' he went on. 'Although that doesn't mean the ghosts aren't dangerous. They can affect your mind quite badly, if you let them get to you.' His grin showed well-whitened teeth. 'But they keep themselves well away from me.'

I blinked, suddenly realizing that the mists were wonderfully silent, no screaming wraiths anywhere. And if this oddball in the cloak could drive ghosts away, and could see the knife . . .

94

'Then you're magical,' I said warily.

'Indeed,' he nodded. 'Some psychic ability, and quite a considerable share of the higher magic. So if you don't mind . . .'

He murmured a strange word or two, moved a long pale hand oddly. And at once my clothes were repaired and more or less clean.

'Thanks,' I said, still peering at him watchfully.

'A pleasure. Couldn't have you going around like that.' He grinned again. 'And you may put your suspicions to rest, my boy. I'm not Cartel, never have been. And I would guess that you're not . . . ?'

'Definitely not,' I said. 'I'm not magical either.' I saw him glance at the knife again. 'So why are *you* in the mists?'

He looked slightly startled by the question. 'I often leave the path and come exploring, seeking to learn more about the place. My ESP is rather limited, short-range, so I must explore in person.' He smiled. 'Happily, I was near enough to get an ESP glimpse of you, apparently in trouble. Knowing how many horrible creatures lurk and hunt in here, I came to help.' The smile grew a bit uneasy. 'Clearly you didn't need me. Though if you're not magical, I can't work out why your clothes were torn and bloodstained, yet you're unharmed.'

'Just lucky,' I said vaguely. 'And . . . er . . . it wasn't my blood.'

He looked startled again. 'You must be quite a warrior, despite your youth. May I know your name?'

I shrugged. No reason why not. 'Nick Walker.'

He didn't seem to recognize my name, which a Cartel mage might have. 'Pleased to meet you, Nick,' he said. 'I am Bertrand Nowell, an *actor* by profession. You may have heard of me . . . ?'

He was looking hopeful, then slightly crushed when I shook my head. 'Ah, well,' he said. 'My work has mostly been in the theatre. And not really *leading* parts, so much . . .'

'I've been living on the streets most of my life,' I explained. 'Couldn't afford the cinema, let alone the theatre.'

'How sad,' he sighed. 'A homeless waif . . . But you must be more than that to have been consigned to this place.' He peered at me curiously. 'Can you tell me why you're here?'

'I tried to kill a high-powered Cartel mage,' I said, keeping it short. Then I hesitated, still not sure I trusted him. But he was better than nothing, he'd clearly been wandering that place a while and he said he'd come to help me. 'He sent two friends of mine here at the same time,' I went on. 'Any chance you might've seen them? One is the girl I was looking for, about my age, pretty, with long brown hair – and the other's a stocky man with a grey beard . . .'

He shook his head sadly. 'You're the first *living* person I've seen, in the mists or on the Path, for quite some time.'

I sagged a little at that. But still, I thought, he could be useful. At the very least he might give me a few tips about the place. He was the closest thing to an expert that I was likely to find.

'I know this place is called the Downward Path,' I said. 'But – do you know what happens when you get all the way down, to the end?'

'I've never got there, thankfully,' Bertrand said. 'I suspect that one never does. The downward slope is probably an illusion, designed to make people fearful and despairing. I suspect they walk until they die. And then . . . they join the mists.'

I shivered. That wasn't much of an alternative. But I had another, more crucial question.

'You said you'd seen other living people, some time ago,' I said. 'Can you tell me how you did it? And . . . would you help me look for my friends?'

'I'm not unwilling to help you, Nick,' he said, still looking sad. 'But you mustn't have false hopes. The Path is immeasurably long, made so by the Cartel's magic. And that magic also seems to ensure that if you return to the Path after being in the mists, you never get back to the same spot you left. Nor can you then go back to the place in the mists that you just left.' He shook his head. 'It's all totally random, possibly designed to be part of the torment.'

'Then how did you find those others?' I asked.

'Pure accident,' he said. 'Moving from the mists on to the Path at a place where someone happened to be. For instance, a while ago I came on to the Path and found a woman walking there. I must have frightened her, for she ran off before I could speak to her, and I couldn't catch up. Ever since, I've wished my ESP was more powerful. Because, though I've tried to find her again, I never have.'

I wasn't as sympathetic as he probably hoped. The story had speeded up my pulse-rate for another reason. 'Did you see what she looked like?' I asked urgently.

'She wasn't your girl, if that's what you're thinking,' he said. 'An older blonde, thin but attractive in a slightly washed-out way.'

My pulse still throbbed. That more or less described Julia. 'And you're sure you couldn't find her again?'

He shook his head again. 'I'm very sorry, Nick, but it would have to be another happy accident. It might take *years* of random trial-and-error before you or I came out of the mists on to the right part of the Path, where she was walking.'

I stared at the cold seething paleness around me. If

that was so, if it had to be done the hard way, by random searching, that's what I'd do. Get back to the Path, step off it into the mists, come out on to the Path again, over and over. Coming on to a different part of the Path each time.

And I'd do it for years, if I had to. Because sometime I might accidentally blunder on to a place where one of my friends was walking.

And then I'd have to do it all over again for each of the other three . . .

I didn't let myself think that they too might have left the Path for some reason and found themselves facing monsters in the mists. Sam and April could surely look after themselves, maybe even Paddy could – but Julia wouldn't have a chance.

Still, I thought, it'd be good if I could do my random searching in the company of someone else. Someone with experience of the mists, with at least short-range ESP and with the power to keep the ghosts away . . .

'I'm still going to try to find my friends,' I said. 'As long as there's any hope. So, er, Bertrand . . . will you help? Will you come with me?'

Again, oddly, he glanced at the knife, then looked at me with a slightly wry smile. 'Why not? For a while, anyway. I think it's fairly close to hopeless, but I don't seem to have much else to do. And it's pleasant to have someone to talk to.'

*

I agreed with that, even though he seemed to want to do most of the talking. But he was entertaining enough, as we went along. And the mists remained happily free of howling ghosts.

But then I stumbled over a mist-hidden lump of stone and grabbed his arm to catch my balance.

The arm felt bone-thin within its sleeve. And it was exactly that.

As I clutched him, he jerked away in alarm, and his cloak swirled half-open – to reveal the white fleshless ribs and knobbly joints of a *skeleton*.

And as he frantically tried to cover up, the handsome face within the hood grew half-transparent – showing, behind it, the empty-eyed grinning horror of a skull.

'You're one of them!' I gasped. 'You're a *ghost*!'

He stiffened, with his cloak and his face – what had to be the *illusion* of a face – back in place. 'I certainly am not! I have merely been . . . ah . . . *disembodied*. My flesh-and-blood body is very much alive – elsewhere. Which is why I've kept my magic powers, here, when a ghost could not.'

I scowled. 'You might have said . . .'

'But then you might have fled from me,' he said. 'As you probably will, now.'

'No,' I said quickly. 'It doesn't bother me.' As long as you keep the cloak on, I thought, and keep the face hiding your skull. 'And I do need your help.'

So we set off again, with Bertrand glum and less talkative. 'How long have you been here?' I asked, to break the silence.

'Years, I think,' he sighed. 'Although time, I believe, moves differently on the Path than in the real world . . .'

He paused suddenly, his face seeming to tighten.

'What?' I asked, tightening up myself.

'My ESP can sense something . . . fearful,' he breathed. 'Other living beings in the mists, not far ahead. And someone in even *worse* trouble than you were.'

19

Other living beings . . . Maybe my friends.

I launched into a wild sprint, nearly falling headlong over unseen rubble in the mist, but not slowing down. Bertrand seemed to be trying to hurry too, but managed only long, slow, loping strides, as if that was all a skeleton's legs could do.

'Can you tell who it is?' I yelled back at him as I ran. 'Or if they're male or female?'

'Sorry,' he panted. 'I can only sense their presence . . .'

He fell farther behind as I raced on. And since I was alone again, the ghosts swarmed back at me. But this time they weren't screaming with hatred and fury.

Instead, their voices all blended together in a harsh breathy jerky sound – and it took me a moment, as I ran, to recognize it.

They were *laughing*. Eerie, evil, gloating laughter.

I heard Bertrand's voice, calling from the depths of the mists behind me. 'Wait, Nick! Be careful! There's something *terrible* ahead!'

I didn't turn or reply, just kept running. 'Something *terrible*' could be more grisly monsters, on the attack. I wasn't waiting for anything.

I stopped thinking about Bertrand then, just as I stopped caring whether the ghosts laughed or cried or burst into song. My mind closed against everything but the thought of someone in trouble nearby. And though *four* of my friends were in that ghastly realm, and I wasn't proud of myself for thinking it, I found myself hoping desperately that it wasn't April.

But it was.

In another moment or two the laughing wraith-shapes in the mists drew away from me again, just as a thick bank of mist blinded me. I slowed to a nervy jog, listening hard. An unusually heavy mist could well hold some sort of trap. And that could be what the ghosts found so funny.

Then I suddenly lurched out on to the edge of a broad open area. It held no mist at all, so I could see clearly what it did hold. And none of it was funny.

In that clearing were four people I recognized, and a stranger.

Three of the people were ghosts, semi-transparent with the usual slightly twisted, distorted faces. Ghosts of the three sorcerers – Viney, Blist and Dyer – who had joined Fray in torturing me at Redman's house, until April brought the house down on top of them.

The fourth person, to my horror, was April.

She wasn't a ghost, and seemed unhurt, but she was definitely in trouble. She was motionless and silent, wide-eyed and pale – and magically held floating in the air, lying horizontally so her long hair hung down to the ground.

And the stranger, standing in front of her, was a tall man wearing a long, black, high-collared coat and dark trousers. He had thick, shiny black hair, with deep-set eyes under heavy brows in a strong-boned face.

But it was the face of a devil.

Its skin was creased and leathery, livid with shades of blue and green endlessly rippling and flowing across it. The eyes were glittering ovals of scarlet with no pupils – short, sharp, blue-black horns jutted from the brow – bright fangs glinted in the red-lipped mouth as he grinned at April.

I saw on the edge of my vision that all the ghosts had gathered around like an audience, silent now, also grinning eagerly. But I wasn't concerned with them.

The devil-faced man turned his grin on me, and moved a hand – hairy and clawed, with the same lurid colours moving on its skin. A magical power gripped me like huge invisible clamps and held me still.

'Excellent,' devil-face said, the grin widening. His

voice was an ugly rasp, as cruel as his eyes. 'The Changeless Boy has come to me, saving me the trouble of seeking him.'

The ghosts of the three mages murmured with vicious joy.

'Did you think to gallop to the girl's rescue?' the man went on. 'With your helpful friend, the bony play-actor?'

He paused as if waiting for a reply, so I knew his magical grip must have left me able to speak. But I just stared at him silently.

'Sadly, the play-actor is running and hiding like a rabbit,' the man went on. 'He knows me, you see. As you will come – briefly – to know me.'

He took a step forward, polished boots crunching on small stones. But I didn't need that proof to be sure he wasn't another ghost. Bertrand had said ghosts couldn't do magic, and devil-face could. Whoever he was, he was solidly *there*.

So he could be killed, I thought, if I can get to him.

Or if April can.

'I am Mr Kannis,' the devil-faced man was saying. 'I hold a high-level position in the Cartel, the same ex-ecutive level as the late and not very lamented Mr Redman, whom you met. But you will not escape *me*. No icy demon will appear to carry *me* off.'

Smug and full of himself like them all, I thought, still watching silently. And now a lot of them are dead.

Kannis was chortling quietly, a sound like something scaly dragged across stone. 'Mr Fray's notion of sending you and your friends here – alive, with your powers intact – was notably ill-advised. As so many of his recent actions have been. Yet his blunder has proved unexpectedly useful. This realm is an ideal place to deal with you all, permanently, and I have been sent to do just that. This is Cartel property, and *nothing* can happen here that I do not permit.'

Again he paused, but again I stayed silent, the Cartel had made similarly sweeping arrogant statements in the past – not all of which proved to have any substance. As I had hoped, this seemed to irritate him. He probably wanted me to be howling in terror, begging to be spared.

In his dreams.

'What *will* happen,' Kannis snarled, fangs flashing, 'is that I will do what others should have done long before this. In a short while you will die, and all your Changelessness will not save you. I might even restore some physical ability to these three –' he gestured at the three sorcerers – 'so *they* can have the pleasure of killing you. Painfully.'

The three hazy forms stirred. They had been looking unhappy, since as powerless ghosts they couldn't pick up where they left off with April and me. 'Master,' they moaned, wraith-voices filled with gratitude and blood-lust.

'As for your other friends, who are on the Path,' Kannis went on, 'that fool of a mage, the second-rate psychic and his Powerless woman – all three will accompany you into death. And your ghosts can all remain together, here in these mists – where I'm sure they'll be made welcome.'

The audience of ghosts around us whispered with evil laughter.

'But first,' Kannis hissed, 'there is this remarkable young lady. From the outset the Cartel has sought to corrupt her mind and enslave her considerable powers to serve us. But those who dealt with her before handled her *far* too gently. So she was able to resist – and break free, not once but twice.'

The three sorcerer-ghosts moaned again, remembering their own deaths.

'My plan, however, is more straightforward,' Kannis went on. 'I intend simply to *shatter* her mind. Do you understand? Her ordinary *thinking* processes, along with her will and memory and all the rest, will simply be crushed and destroyed beyond repair. But I shall do that in such a way that her extraordinary *magical* powers remain quite intact.'

'No!' I choked before I could stop myself, struggling uselessly against the magic that gripped me.

'Oh yes,' Kannis grinned. 'It will be a delicate operation, especially since she has a strong young mind that will seek to protect itself. But you can be sure I will succeed. In a few moments, before you die, you will see your girlfriend as she will be for the rest of her life. As obedient as a well-trained dog when we wish to make use of her powers. But otherwise a nearly mindless, helpless, drooling imbecile.'

20

I went on struggling, but the magical grip held me firmly. And Kannis, turning away from me with another chortle, loomed over April. As he raised his blue-green hands I saw more of a glow along his fingers, and his eyes glinted a deeper crimson.

And April, still magically silenced, began to writhe and twist where she lay in mid–air. Her hands clenched into white-knuckled fists – her mouth opened wide in a soundless scream – her back arched as if in a spasm of agony.

'*April!*' I screamed, as I had once before, trying to waken the furies within her.

But if she heard me she showed no response. The ghosts all howled at me with foul laughter, and Kannis's fangs flashed as he grinned. I saw a sheen of sweat on his horned forehead as he hurled his power at her mind. I could almost imagine that evil magic like a deadly firestorm among her brain cells, searing, blasting, crushing, shattering . . .

Even so, he'd said he intended to leave her psychic powers intact. And I would have given anything then to break out of my invisible bonds and free those powers, so she could defend herself. But I had no idea how to do it.

Sam might have known how, but he was far away, lost on the Downward Path. There was no one but me to help April, and I could only watch helplessly and weep as she suffered.

Her body was thrashing and vibrating, by then, for Kannis wasn't only assaulting her mind. I watched her very shape being magically attacked, in vile and horrible ways. Kannis's magic stretched her agonizingly, then crushed her, then twisted and wrung her. I saw her start bleeding from every pore, saw her skin become black and crusty as if charred in an unseen flame. And while she screamed in endless silent anguish I screamed along with her.

And the ghosts howled with joy, and Kannis chortled, and I would have traded the whole rest of my life to be able to move for two seconds, to get to him and kill him. Before those evil torments killed her.

Kannis had planned to keep her alive, but it looked like he was going too far. As Cartel mages often did when offered a chance to hurt someone.

But then, I thought bleakly, April might prefer that. Might prefer to die there, rather than live as a brain-dead slave. And if she did, and Kannis then killed me, she and I would be together – even if we were doomed to stay in those horror-mists.

And Kannis would have failed, and would be punished.

I heard him snarl with new effort, saw him grimace and clench his jaw, saw the redness flare more brightly in his eyes. Suddenly a thin thread of that redness flared out, stretching towards April – and stabbing with horrible ease into her forehead.

In the next instant I knew that Kannis had finally, definitely, gone too far.

But not at all in the way I expected.

April's agonized, flailing movements suddenly stopped. Her silence ended just as suddenly, and her gasping cry would have made me jump if I could have moved.

With the gasp, the red cord reaching from Kannis disappeared, and a golden brightness filled April's eyes.

And as Kannis twitched and stiffened, his own eyes widening, she rose smoothly until she was upright, still in mid-air. Looking completely unharmed, without a mark on her skin or a bloodstain on her clothes.

'No,' Kannis croaked. 'This is not possible . . . You *cannot* . . .'

His fangs flashed with demonic fury, and his hands

111

took on a more lurid glow as he reached out. But April's eyes shone more brightly, with a fury of her own.

A stream of blue-green energy from the sorcerer's hands lanced towards her. But it flowed harmlessly around her, as if she was inside a protective sphere.

Then she moved her hand, almost casually, and Kannis burst into flame.

Screaming, he staggered back. But his own magic doused the flames at once, and he gathered himself to strike again. And I saw April flinch slightly, as if startled by his recovery, as if suddenly unsure of herself.

But while Kannis had been ablaze, deeply shocked by her attack and totally focused on protecting himself, his magical control over *other* things had slipped.

The invisible clamps had let go of me. And he hadn't noticed.

Before he could deliver his next magic, I leaped forward, moving as fast as I ever have in my life, and drove the knife deep into his side.

He screamed again, and his power hurled me wildly away, across the breadth of the clearing. I landed hard on the stony ground, feeling my elbow shatter and my collarbone snap.

Kannis was swaying and bleeding but still standing, so I knew I'd only wounded him. But he didn't have a chance to do anything more to me. And the agony from my broken bones didn't keep me from seeing the moment when April's hand moved again in a slashing sweep.

As another eruption of searing flame blazed up around him, Kannis simply vanished, like a burst bubble.

April started to turn to me, still looking startled and a little fearful. Then her eyes rolled up so only the whites showed, and she crumpled to the ground.

21

I struggled to my feet, forcing myself, as usual, to ignore the pain. The clearing was still silent, since all the ghosts – including the three sorcerers – had fled into the mists when Kannis vanished. Hobbling over to April, I knelt beside her, feeling a rush of relief that she was breathing normally.

I realized she'd probably just fainted, maybe from overexertion. It had been a really impressive display. And her amazing psychic powers had done a good job of self-healing too, since even close up I didn't see a mark on her.

Then I glimpsed a dark shape in the mists and stood up, heart pounding, knife ready. Most of my pain was gone by then, the broken bones nearly restored, but that wouldn't help me if Kannis was back.

But he wasn't. It was Bertrand in his hooded cloak, sidling into the clear area, looking a bit shamefaced. And peering curiously at April.

'Nick, dear boy,' he said. 'How wonderful to find you alive!'

'Yeah, right,' I said. 'Lucky me. And lucky *you*, keeping well out of it.'

The image of his face flickered briefly, the skull-grin showing through. 'I'm deeply sorry about that,' he murmured. 'But . . . Kannis simply terrifies me.'

I couldn't blame him for that. 'Me too,' I said with a shrug.

'But you were so *brave*,' he said. 'And the girl . . .' He peered intently at her again. 'You didn't tell me she was magical.'

I didn't tell you lots of things, I thought.

'Quite amazing,' Bertrand went on. 'Does she have psychic powers as well?'

I blinked. 'That's *all* she has. She doesn't have any of the other . . .'

'The higher magic?' He looked puzzled. 'My dear Nick, that's what she was *using*! Quite wild and uncontrolled, but very strong!'

'She couldn't have,' I said, frowning. 'She never has . . .'

'Really?' Bertrand raised an eyebrow. 'I don't think I'm mistaken.'

I was still frowning. 'It looked like her PK when she sent Kannis away.'

'She didn't,' Bertrand said, startling me again. 'You'd

hurt Kannis badly, and your friend was wielding that fire . . . He took himself away.' His sudden laugh was full of joy. 'Be proud, Nick! The two of you made *Kannis* run!'

'I'd rather have made him dead,' I muttered, 'because he'll probably be back.'

I sheathed the knife – noticing Bertrand peering at it again with that odd look – then stooped and picked April up. My injuries had recovered and she was small and slim, not much of a weight. 'Now, can you get me back to the Path?'

He seemed willing enough, and we set off through the silent mists. I knew that the ghosts were still around somewhere, along with assorted demons. And that empty inhuman place was never going to be *peaceful*. But right then I was just grateful for the quiet and didn't worry about the rest of it.

I'd found April, she was alive, and there was a good chance that when she came around – if it *was* just a faint – her mind would be as unharmed as her body.

But also, as I followed Bertrand, I was wondering if it might be true that she *had* somehow suddenly got some of those other powers, the higher magic. That could make a huge difference.

It might help us find our other friends. But more – it might even help us to find a way to escape . . .

I made myself smother that thought. I never liked

tempting fate. And to help push those near-impossible dreams away, I triggered Bertrand's love of talking, especially about himself.

'You've met Kannis before, then, have you?' I asked him.

'Sadly, yes,' he said, with a tremor in his voice. 'It was he who took my body from me and sent me to this hateful limbo.'

'Was it?' I said, keeping my voice neutral. I still wasn't sure I believed a lot of what Bertrand said. He still could be a part of the Cartel, being punished for some reason by being sent to the Path. 'Why did he do that?'

He turned to face me, drawing himself up. 'Because,' he intoned in his most stagy voice, 'I refused to betray someone I once loved.'

'Very heroic,' I muttered, still walking on. 'I hope she appreciated it.' Or maybe it was a *he*, I thought.

And then he staggered me as if he'd hit me with a club.

'Manta?' he said, with a bitter laugh. 'She probably never knew about it. And if she did, she *certainly* wouldn't care.'

I nearly dropped April with the shock of it, and it took me several seconds of gasping before I found my voice.

'*Manta*?' I said, almost shouting the name. '*Manta* is the someone you loved?'

He blinked at me, puzzled. 'Actually, I was *married* to her.'

That shocked me all over again, and whatever showed on my face made him draw back uneasily. 'What is it?' he asked. 'Do you know her?'

'*Know* her?' I was still yelling. 'It's *her* fault that the Cartel keeps on trying to kill me! It's mostly because of her that I've ended up *here*, with my friends!'

'I can believe that,' he said. 'What exactly did she do?'

I opened my mouth to yell at him again, but stopped. I wanted to find out about him, not tell him about me.

'It's a long story,' I muttered. 'You said you *were* married – did she dump you?'

'Certainly not,' he sniffed. 'I left *her*.'

I didn't much care if that was true. I had a more important question. 'And when you were married – did you have a child?'

'No,' he said, sounding oddly wary. 'Why do you ask?'

'Just wondering,' I said. 'Anyway, when you refused to betray her to the Cartel, that must have been after you left her?'

'Nearly four years after that, yes,' he said. 'I thought

118

she'd lost her mind when I started hearing about her attacks on them. And before long Kannis came to me, offering a reward if I helped the Cartel find her. It was clear that they wanted to kill her, and I couldn't let that happen. I was still . . . fond of her. So I refused.'

And got yourself turned into a skeleton and sent to the Downward Path, I thought. Maybe that *was* heroic.

But then the conversation ended, as with unexpected suddenness Bertrand grabbed my shoulder and we stepped out of the mists into the corridor of clear air along the Path – together.

'We haven't been separated?' I said.

'No. If we are touching, we stay together.'

I digested this new piece of information while I set April down gently. 'When she comes to,' I said to Bertrand, 'we can start looking for my other friends.'

'Not *we*,' Bertrand said. 'I think I'll be on my way.'

I scowled. 'You said you'd help me!'

'I said *for a while*.' He sniffed. 'And I've got you back to the Path. Now . . . I'm sorry, but it won't be safe, being around you, when Kannis comes back.'

In that moment I heard a moan from April and turned quickly towards her. As I did so, I felt the faintest of tugs at my belt. I might not have noticed – except that I'd had experience of pickpockets, on the streets. I knew what it felt like.

I whirled towards Bertrand again, to find him

stalking away in a hurry towards the edge of the Path, and the mists.

With one sleeve of his cloak showing the luminous glow of the knife, clutched in his skeletal hand.

22

I leaped after him, fury moving me as fast as when I attacked Kannis. And urgency too – if I left April to chase Bertrand in the mists I might never get back to her – but I'd be nothing without my knife.

Luckily, as before, Bertrand seemed to have only one pace, so I caught up with him easily on the very edge of the Path. As he turned I saw that stress had again caused him to lose magical control, so the illusion of his face was gone. The hollow-eyed skull-face confronted me, and a hand of bone waved the knife at me.

'Get away!' he said, sounding shaky. 'I must have this knife! I need it more than you do!'

'You have *no idea* how wrong you are,' I snarled. 'What do you need it for?'

Ignoring the question, he tried to scuttle past me, but I moved to block his path. I couldn't guess how strong his bony form might be, but it definitely wasn't quick.

Just desperate, for some reason.

'Leave me alone!' he cried. 'Or I'll *hurt* you!'

'You don't have a body,' I spat through my teeth. 'You can't hurt me.'

I hadn't forgotten that he was magical. I was trying to rattle him, get him off balance. And it worked. When I made a lunge to grab him, he had no time to throw magic at me.

Instead, he did just what I hoped. Frantically, he stabbed at me with the golden blade.

I was quick enough to get an arm in the way. And it was a fairly weak thrust, so not much more than the point sank into my flesh.

I grabbed the rest of the blade in my other hand – ignoring the pain as the razor edges sliced my fingers – and yanked the hilt out of his bony grasp.

He cried out, a whiny sound like a spoiled child being deprived of a toy. But I turned away, pulling the blade from my arm, not interested in his reaction. I had the knife back, so I wanted to get back to April and get rid of him, in that order.

But he came creeping after me. And when I heard him gasp, I turned to see his eyes bulging as he stared at my wounds. Where the bleeding was already slowing, the cuts starting to close up.

With an awkward rush that made me brace myself for another attack, he flung himself in front of me. But he was looking shocked, not aggressive. And he was staring at my throat.

'The Mark . . .' he breathed. 'I hadn't noticed it before . . . Oh, gods – Manta made you *changeless*!'

I scowled. 'You know the Mark?'

'Indeed I do.' Another bitter laugh. 'I pleaded with her, more times than I could count, to place that spell on me. *Begged* her!'

I couldn't believe it. 'Why on earth would you want it?'

'I'm an actor,' he said, as if it was the most obvious reason in the world. 'Can you imagine what it would mean, never ageing, never changing? I could go on working indefinitely! I could become a *star*!'

I almost laughed. But I supposed he was right. For someone who could avoid upsetting the Cartel, being changeless wouldn't be so much of a curse as it was for me. 'Why wouldn't she do it?' I asked, curious.

He sniffed. 'She said her powers weren't to be used for trivial and selfish reasons. But *she* was the selfish one . . . That was one of the reasons why I left her.'

In fact I could see Manta's point. 'You're a mage though,' I said. 'Couldn't you do the spell for yourself?'

'It's a rare and secret piece of witchery, from that special book of hers,' he said, looking mournful. 'I could never find the spell anywhere else. And any other spells like it all came with a price. With one of them you'd stay unchanged for decades – and then suddenly turn to dust or fade away to nothing.'

Nasty, I thought. Given the choice, I'd take Manta's spell. But I'd lost interest in Bertrand and his problems.

'Right, so now you can do some fading away,' I told him. 'From me. I don't want to have to watch my back with you creeping around after the knife.'

'Oh, no, I wouldn't . . .' he began. But then he saw my disbelief and shut up, drooping unhappily.

'Anyway, why *do* you want it?' I asked, repeating the question that he'd ignored before. 'What good is it to you?'

'It's . . . ah . . . the *colour*, dear boy,' he said, trying to smile. 'Such an antidote to the grey miseries of this place.'

'Really,' I said, not believing him for a second, no longer caring. 'But I need it to help keep me *alive*, here or anywhere. So clear off. And stay away from me.'

He peered at me woefully, glanced longingly at the knife, then sighed and turned away. In a moment his cloaked shape was swallowed up by the mists.

And then, at last, I got back to April. To find her sitting up, looking a bit woozy but wearing a smile that seemed to outshine the knife-blade.

'Whoever was that . . . person, in the cloak?' she asked.

'Not important – tell you later,' I said, crouching beside her. 'Are you all right?'

'I think so,' she said. 'Thanks to you, coming to my rescue. Again.'

'I'm not sure you really needed me,' I said.

'*I'm* sure,' she told me, getting slowly to her feet.

I watched her, worrying. 'So all those tortures and everything that Kannis did to you didn't . . . damage you at all?'

'I think they were mostly illusions, to terrify me,' she said. 'Except what he was doing inside my head . . .'

'That definitely hurt you,' I said, still worried. 'Didn't it?'

'Yes, a lot. But it was worth it.' Her hazel eyes were shining along with her smile. 'Kannis made a big mistake, Nick. He was trying to shatter my mind – but all he managed to do was break down that second barrier in my mind that Paddy found! Suddenly I had all that new power, that I didn't really understand . . . But along with that, I've got my memory back! I can remember *everything*!'

23

'Everything?' I repeated, stunned.

'Just about,' she said happily. She seemed a lot more pleased about having her memory back than about the new unnerving magic she'd got. 'Not stuff from when I was very little – no one can remember their earliest years. And there might be a few other gaps.' She grinned. 'But now I know my full name – April Slater. And I turned fourteen in September.'

When she was a street kid, I thought. A month before I found her. 'Do you remember your parents at all?' I asked carefully.

'Not in any detail. I remember my mother just as sort of a vague, warm, loving shape – and I don't remember anything about my father.' The happy glow on her face darkened. 'My earliest *clear* memory is screaming my heart out when the Cartel came and kidnapped me, the first time.'

My insides twisted as I imagined the scene – the toddler torn out of her mother's arms by whatever mages and monsters had been sent to take her . . .

126

And I twitched again when I noticed that the Path had taken hold of us, in its way, and without realizing we'd started walking.

'I think they killed my mother then too,' she murmured. '*Elg* was there, Nick, with some sorcerers, including Fray. And Elg had blood on her claws . . .'

She would, I thought bitterly, remembering the foul vampirish woman who had tormented both April and me at Redman's house. But I didn't think they *had* killed April's mother – and I was about to say so, but stopped myself. It wasn't the best time to bring up my notions about April and Manta.

'Elg is *here* too,' April was saying. 'Her ghost came to me on the Path, told me you were being held by other ghosts, being tortured in the mists . . .'

So she had been lured in, just as I had. To where Kannis was waiting.

'I don't think the ghosts can do that,' I said.

'Maybe not – but they can do enough. Especially to a psychic. They got at me through my ESP, all that shrieking and ranting and hating, till I thought my head would explode.' Her eyes darkened. 'I thought it would with Kannis too. And it was the same kind of pain, a mental agony, that happened to me in all those years with the Cartel, in some big gloomy house . . .'

She described years of being a prisoner, while they poked around in her mind and pressured her in different ways, trying to control her will, trying to make her one of them. But she held out against them, strengthened by her deep anger at how she had been kidnapped and what they had done.

Until at last they put the barriers in her mind and robbed her of her memories. And of her powers as well, which by then were probably starting to show.

But still she didn't break, didn't give in, fighting everything that they threw at her to make her their slave. Until at last an uncontrolled burst of her PK erupted through the barrier, like the ones she produced when I first met her. Enough for her to find a way out of that place – to freedom, if not safety.

'It's almost funny,' I muttered, not smiling. 'They keep trying to crush you, and every time they just wake up your powers. And this time they've stirred up the *higher* magic in you. That'll shock them.' Then I did smile a little. 'It definitely shocked Kannis.'

She peered at me. 'How did you know what it was? I thought it was my PK, at first.'

'The person in the cloak told me,' I said. 'He's a sort of mage . . .' I quickly told her about Bertrand, but without mentioning Manta.

'But it was like when my psychic powers first burst out,' she said. 'What I did to Kannis just *happened*. I didn't have any *control*. It's really frustrating – I can sense the magic in me, but I can't reach it or take hold

128

of it.'

'That's bad news,' I muttered. 'You were sort of super-powerful back there. I was hoping that with *both* sorts of magic, you might find a way out of here.'

'I wouldn't know where to start.' She sighed. 'We need Sam – he's got both sorts too.'

'Then let's find him,' I said. 'And Paddy and Julia.'

'Are they really here?' she asked.

I nodded. 'Bertrand once saw a woman that must have been Julia. She and Paddy probably got separated, like we did.'

'So they've both been alone, all this time . . .' Her voice trembled – but then she frowned. 'How did this Bertrand manage to see Julia? I found that the Path somehow blocks ESP. Ever since I got here, as I walked along, I've been reaching out psychically for you and Sam. But I just met . . . blankness.'

'Bertrand said he found her by accident,' I said. 'It seems you can get from one bit of the Path to another by going into the mists and coming out again. You always come out at a different spot. And if that's the only way to look for them, we'll have to do it too.' I grimaced. 'The problem is – it's totally random. It could be ages before we got lucky and came out at the place where they are. Or it could never happen at all.'

Still, April agreed that there was no other way. And because she was determined and brave, she refused to worry about the effect that the haunted mists could have on her extra-sensitive psychic mind.

'If Kannis and all the other Cartel sorcerers couldn't drive me crazy,' she said tightly, 'I don't think a few wispy spooks will. Let's go.'

She turned towards the edge of the Path, and I followed. 'That's the trouble,' I reminded her. 'There's not just a *few*.' Then a thought struck me. 'But it could be that now, with your new powers, they'll be afraid of you! They took off in a hurry after you blasted Kannis – and they've always stayed clear of Bertrand. Maybe they're scared of mages who aren't Cartel!'

'Then we won't tell them I can't control my magic,' she said.

It was clear, though, that she *wanted* to find some control. As we held on to each other and stepped back into the mists to begin our search, she was frowning and gritting her teeth. But then she slumped, looking defeated.

'I was trying to make a flame,' she said. 'But I can't. It's all just out of reach.'

'You flamed Kannis pretty well,' I said.

She shrugged. 'That just burst out by itself – probably because I was in danger.'

No shortage of that here in the mists, I thought, remembering the horror-creatures I'd faced. Then I realized that I hadn't told April about those battles, and

I gave her a brief account – so we could both be on our guard.

But it seemed, as we warily walked on, that we were in a monster-free area. And I remembered before, when I'd met Bertrand and then when I ran to find April – and after that, going back to the Path . . . No monsters.

Maybe the monsters, I thought, knew enough to keep away from those with magic powers. Like the ghosts did.

I just felt grateful for small mercies, as we turned back towards the Path.

We hadn't gone very far into the mists, so it was easy to retrace our steps. And I suppose we were both thinking about what we might find when we got back on to the Path at a different spot. But even so we stayed alert. So we both glimpsed the dark shape creeping through the mists ahead.

We stopped, I drew the knife, April reached out with an ESP scan . . .

But what loomed out of the mists in front of us wasn't Kannis, or a demon. It was Bertrand. Again.

I relaxed slightly, keeping the knife ready. 'What now?'

He was peering at April as before, but turned to me with a sniff. 'I've come to *warn* you,' he said. 'There's something horrible in the mists . . .'

'I know,' I said. 'A lot of ghosts and monsters, and one skeleton.'

He glared. 'I'm talking about something *new*. An enormous evil creature that isn't afraid of mages, like the other creatures are. And it seems to be *hunting*. Most probably for you.'

24

That shook me. Had Kannis sent a special new demon stalker after April and me? Or, I suddenly wondered, was this a lie, some plot of Bertrand's?

'Nice of you to come and tell us,' I said, with some sarcasm.

'Not really,' he snapped. 'I want to make a deal. I know the mists well, and I can help you keep away from the monster. In exchange for the knife.'

'Not a chance,' I said at once.

'We can look after ourselves,' April added, eyes flashing.

'Against this new thing? I wonder,' Bertrand said coldly. 'Still, do as you like. I'll just take the knife from your corpse.' And he turned and vanished into the mists.

April's face twisted as we stumbled on. 'Do you think he was telling the truth?'

I shrugged. 'If there is something hunting us, I can't

see how Bertrand could help us hide from it. It was probably just a feeble trick to get the knife.'

'Why does he want it?'

'He says it's for the glow, but I think that's a lie.' I shrugged. 'Though I can't think what his real reason could be. And I don't plan to find out the hard way.'

We set off again, back towards the Path. Around us the drifting mists seemed to get thicker, making us trip and stumble. So we slowed down. We knew that if we hurt ourselves April could heal herself and I'd get restored. But it wouldn't be good to be waiting for a sprained ankle to get better when a big new monster found us.

In a while, though, the mists thinned out again, showing no sign of a monster anywhere. And I was feeling more certain that Bertrand had lied when April came to a sudden stop, her fingers taking a painful grip on my arm.

'*There*,' she gasped, pointing to the wall of mist that we'd just left. 'Something huge, and horrible . . . and aware of us . . .'

I drew the knife and braced myself, staring at the bank of mist, as April let go of me and steeled herself as well.

And then I saw how overmatched we were.

The monstrosity heaving into view looked like an

immense boulder, roughly dome-shaped, the size of a moving van. But it was a living, moving creature, covered in ridged dark-grey skin like thick armour.

It had no visible head, but at the front of the dome I saw a number of large dark bumps like monster-sized warts, as well as four glassy circles that might have been eyes. And below all that was the enormously wide thin slit of a giant lipless mouth.

When it spotted us, the mouth began to open slightly, as if hungrily. Oddly, I saw only darkness inside that wide opening – no sign of teeth or other weapons.

I knew it would have something to attack with though, and I was in no hurry to find out what it might be.

Where the dome-shape touched the ground its edges rippled and flowed, so that it looked a bit like a vast, humped, swollen slug slithering through the mists. Moving a lot faster than I liked.

Still, April's ESP had given us that useful warning, and it was some distance away. So we ran.

At full pelt we were faster than the monster, but that only helped for a while. April could sense it coming steadily after us, and I was grimly sure that it wasn't about to give up and stop. It wouldn't tire as quickly as we would, maybe not at all. And the treacherous, uneven ground wasn't troubling it a bit.

'Can you do anything?' I panted, glancing at April. 'PK or something?'

'I tried that as soon as I saw it,' she gasped. 'But it seems to be shielded, more strongly than Fray's monsters were.'

My heart sank. I knew there wasn't much that the knife and I could do to an oversized armoured slug either.

But then I realized that even if we couldn't fight it or outrun it, we might have a way to hide.

'When we get back to the Path,' I said, 'we have to get straight off again, which should get us back into a different part of the mists. And then we'll get *on* again, to a different part of the Path.'

'All right,' she said. 'But it's stalking us, Nick. And it found us once . . . I wish Sam was here.'

Sam plus the SAS, I thought. Then we put our heads down, held hands tightly, and ran.

We were still in that headlong sprint, though close to running out of steam, when we burst out on to the Path. Our momentum nearly took us all the way across and over the other edge into the lightless void, but we managed to stop in time.

As ever, the Path was silent and deserted. Also as ever, while we stood there shakily, puffing and panting, the magic took hold of us and started us walking.

136

'It wasn't so far behind,' April said, peering warily back at the mists. 'Do you think it'll come on to the Path after us?'

'I don't know,' I said. 'Maybe the randomness would take it on to another bit.' Or maybe, I thought, I don't know what I'm talking about.

'And if we go back into the mists,' she went on, 'are you *sure* we'll go into a different bit? Not just back where we were? Where it is?'

I shook my head. 'I'm not sure of anything. But if the magic does bring us to a different place whenever we come *out* of the mists, on to the Path, there's a good chance that it works the other way as well.'

'A *chance*,' she repeated, giving me a look.

'The other option,' I pointed out, 'is just to stay here and keep aimlessly walking. With no hope of finding our friends. Until the monster finds us.'

'No.' She managed a faint smile. 'The *real* option is just to be ready to run.'

'Good plan,' I said.

And we turned together, keeping a connection between us all the time, and stepped back into the mists.

With relief, I found that the randomness apparently did work both ways. We saw no sign of the huge monster at the spot where we'd re-entered the mists. And April's ESP picked up no sense of its presence.

'So it worked,' she said, smiling. 'Your off-the-Path-on-again trick.'

'Nick's tricks never fail,' I said lightly. 'So now while we're looking for the others we'll also be staying clear of the monster.'

She grinned. 'That means the magic of this place is actually *helping* us. And have you noticed how we're not getting hungry? We probably won't get sleepy either. As if the magic has shut down all our normal . . . body functions.'

'Just as well,' I muttered. 'I forgot the loo paper.'

That made her giggle. 'But that helps too. We won't have to stop for *anything*. We can just keep going, keep searching.' She laughed again. 'Wouldn't the Cartel be furious if they knew their magic was being *helpful*?'

That changed the mood, for me, and I glanced edgily around. 'Let's hope they don't find out,' I said, 'or we'll have more than a big ugly monster to try to hide from.'

April's smile faded, and she also glanced nervously around.

And then she screamed.

Just as a dark bulky shape erupted suddenly out of the mists and grabbed my left wrist in a crushing grip.

25

I couldn't break that grip to draw the knife, so I twisted around and started a wild kick . . .

To find myself staring at Sam.

'Sorry about that, lad,' he said, letting me go, patting my shoulder. 'Didn't want you usin' that knife before you knew it was me.'

I just stared at him, amazed beyond speech, while April made a sound somewhere between a sob and a laugh of relief and flung her arms around him.

He hugged her hard for a moment. 'Never expected to find you two *together*, in this God-awful place.'

'We never expected to be found,' I muttered. 'Were you looking for us?'

'Every minute since I got here,' Sam said. 'What're you doin' in the mists?'

'Trying to find you,' April said, 'and Paddy and Julia.'

'And this is the way to get from one part of the Path to another,' I added.

'Worked that out, did you?' Sam said. 'That's how I've been searchin' for you.'

'I was told,' I said, and quickly told him about Bertrand.

Sam frowned. 'A mage who's an actor . . . Sounds familiar, but I never met him. Hard luck on him, bein' here.'

I might have said more, about Bertrand and Manta and all the rest, but Sam had more urgent concerns. 'Anyway, it's not safe in the mists – and not just because of the ghosts. There's—'

'A horrible monster,' April broke in again. 'Like an enormous slug.'

'We've seen it,' I said. 'We dodged on to the Path to lose it.'

'Way ahead of me, aren't you?' Sam grinned. 'But I can't work out why the thing is *here*. It's Cartel-made, but it's not a creature that belongs here. The Path's a place of *punishment*, where the Cartel's enemies are sent to suffer. Why send a demon stalker? Some folk on the Path might be glad to be put out of their misery.'

'I think the monster was sent after us,' I said. 'By a sorcerer named Kannis.'

Sam stiffened. '*Kannis?* What's he got to do with you?'

Then his mouth fell open as April and I quickly told

140

him about her capture, and the fight with Kannis after he had accidentally freed her higher magic.

'Shows how even high-level mages can be stupid,' Sam said with an amazed grin. 'That second barrier in your mind, blockin' your higher magic *and* your memory, would've been put in when you were little. Before your magic really started developin'. But now those powers must've been fightin' to break out – and whatever Kannis did in your head opened the way!' He laughed merrily. 'Wonder how he'll explain that world-class blunder to the rest of the Cartel!'

'It's even funnier,' I said, 'because Kannis was sneering at *Fray* for blundering, sending us here.'

Sam laughed again. 'He's not wrong. The Cartel wouldn't be pleased that we were sent here alive and with all our powers, and Nick with his knife . . . Fray'll be in worse trouble now.'

'Good,' April said.

'Really good,' Sam agreed. 'But then Cartel sorcerers often botch things, when they start thinkin' they're superstars, forgettin' they're not indestructible and can make mistakes. And that can give us an edge, as long as we never forget that *we're* not indestructible either. No matter how much magic we have.'

We both nodded, though Sam was looking at April when we spoke. But he was still grinning.

'And it sounds like you have plenty, lass,' he told her.

'What you did to Kannis was really impressive. I wondered how much of the higher magic you'd have.'

April frowned. 'You said something like that before. What made you think I had any?'

'It was Paddy,' Sam said. 'He thought you must have somethin' really special, more than your psychic ability, to make the Cartel keep comin' after you, tryin' to recruit you . . .'

'But I don't really *have* those other powers,' April sighed. 'With Kannis, it all burst out by itself. I can't *call* on the magic, or control it.'

'You just need to learn the spells and processes and all that,' Sam said. 'I could give you a crash course to get you started, if I had my books and things.'

'Let's nip back and get them,' I muttered.

'Yeah, well, I'm workin' on that,' Sam said. 'But before anythin' else, we have to find Paddy and Julia. And stay out of that monster's way while we look.' He glowered into the mists. 'If it's been set to home in on you two, that explains the *look* of it, the huge mouth . . . It could be more of a *gatherer*, sent to swallow you up alive. Then the spell that put it here would take it back to some Cartel base in our world, to spit you out again.'

And April won't be bringing any power-drills to smash this one, I thought. 'Not the homecoming I had in mind.'

142

'How can it swallow us if we stay away from it?' April asked.

Sam shrugged. 'Chase you down, sneak up on you . . . It'll have some built-in magic that would do the trick.'

'Then we need some magic to keep it off,' I said.

'Except it's *shielded* against magic,' April murmured.

Sam was looking thoughtful. 'It'd be better to get rid of it, or it'll go on gettin' in the way. And the answer to a magic shield is a more powerful magic *weapon*.'

'Could you make one?' April asked, looking hopeful.

'Maybe.' He scowled at the mists again, then waved a hand. 'Let's get back to the Path and start the back-and-forth searchin' for Paddy and Julia. But don't say anythin' for a while. I'll go on thinkin' about a weapon, you keep a lookout for monsters.'

It made quite a difference, I thought, having Sam there as we walked on through the mists. Though April and I stayed watchful, Sam's powerful presence meant that our nerves weren't wound up so tight. It also helped that the ghosts, and all monsters aside from the big new one, were still staying far away.

But after a while I could feel the place getting to me again, because of the new monstrous danger lurking in it. The silence didn't seem welcome any more but heavy and threatening, along with the dank chill, the endless ominous drifting of the mists . . .

I would have given a lot for a glimpse of sunshine. I could understand Bertrand wanting the knife for its golden glow.

Then I felt ashamed, moaning about the creepiness of the place after such a short time. How desperate must Paddy and Julia feel, after walking the Path for weeks?

But that train of thought fell off the rails and I jumped wildly when April elbowed me, pointing behind us.

Turning, I felt a deeper chill as I saw the huge dark dome-shape, some distance away, flowing through the mists towards us at speed.

26

S am turned as well, scowling at the monstrosity as it slithered closer. 'We're not ready to pick a fight with it yet,' he growled, half to himself.

Calmly raising his hands high, he moved them in sweeping curves above the heads of all three of us while growling a stream of strange syllables. For an instant the misty air around us seemed to sparkle with pale-blue light, then was just mist again.

The monster slowed, the vast mouth opening slightly. As we moved quietly away, it surged forward again – towards the place where we'd been.

'We're veiled now,' Sam said. 'It can't see us or sense us while the spell lasts. Let's get to the Path.'

I glanced at the monster, slithering away in the wrong direction, then followed Sam and April. And the wispy edge of a vaguely puzzling thought tried to surface at the back of my mind. Until I got distracted.

'If you can keep us veiled,' April asked Sam, 'why do we need to fight the monster?'

'It's hard to keep a veilin' spell intact over more than one person,' Sam told her. 'Especially when we're movin'. The spell could break down any time.'

'Not good,' I said, 'if Big Slithery is around when it happens.'

'Then do you know how to fight it yet?' April asked.

'I've got half an idea, anyway,' he said. 'Still need to work the bugs out.'

My flesh crawled as I saw mental pictures of a giant worm-thing and a spiky beetle-thing and now a vast slithery slug-thing . . . 'Let's not talk about bugs,' I muttered.

And two steps later we were on the Path.

'Now, then,' Sam said, as the magic started us walking. 'I think I've worked out the kind of weapon we need. And I'm fairly sure I can remember the spell that will make it.'

Just like that, I thought, impressed. And yet even with all that magical power, Sam didn't have any of the arrogance of a Cartel mage. Just an easy confidence . . .

'The trouble is,' he went on, 'I can't work out a safe way to *use* it.'

Maybe not all *that* much confidence.

'What about an unsafe way?' I asked.

'Only if I have to,' he growled, looking unhappy. 'But anyway, I'll make the thing, and you can help think of what to do with it.'

146

He seemed only to glance back at the mists, but his PK reached out and brought what he wanted – a good-sized lump of ordinary rock. But I didn't think the weapon he had in mind was a catapult.

Holding the big rock in one hand, Sam slowly ran his other hand over its craggy surface, as if stroking it, while murmuring the words of a spell that was almost a chant. For a half-second I thought I saw tiny blue flames, almost too small to be visible, rippling across the surface where his hand had been. Then they were gone. But the rock seemed to have swollen slightly, with a blue tinge in its cracks and crevices.

'What is it?' April breathed, looking fascinated.

'You could say it's a bomb,' Sam rumbled. 'Enough to flatten a good-sized village.'

'So it'll kill that monster?' I asked.

'There's the problem,' Sam said, looking gloomy. 'With the shieldin' that the monster has, a *nuclear* bomb wouldn't make a mark on it. But I had a good ESP look at the thing, and I think the Cartel have made the same mistake that Fray did with that big worm-thing you told me about. I think all the protection is on the monster's outside. So – we have to find a way to make it *swallow* our bomb, before I say the word to detonate it.'

'Why not just magic the bomb inside?' I asked. 'Put it in with PK?'

'Couldn't get it past the shieldin',' Sam said. 'Couldn't get the word past either, to set it off. We have to find a way to make the monster open its mouth.'

Like I did with the worm-thing, I thought. And the idea came to me like switching on a light.

'I could get its mouth open,' I announced. 'You said the monster is probably here to gather us up, right? So I'll let it swallow *me*, and take the bomb in with me. Then you can set it off.'

April looked horrified. 'Nick, you'd be *killed*!'

'Most likely just injured,' I said. 'And you know I'll recover.'

Though if someone *has* to die, I thought, I won't let it be April. Or Sam – because without him April and Paddy and Julia could be on the Path forever.

'Maybe you won't have to go that far, Nick,' Sam said. 'When it opens its mouth to gobble you up, you could just *throw* the bomb down its throat. And then we can PK you out of the way.'

That could work, I thought. If it has a throat. If it doesn't grab me too quickly. If Sam's right about the monster's unshielded insides. If it doesn't have some secret magic that we don't know about.

If we see any pigs flying across a blue moon . . .

But there wasn't much point fretting over all the things that could go wrong when there wasn't anything we could do about them. I just hoped that Sam had a Plan B.

Though if things did go wrong, I might not be around to find out what it was.

I stared into the mists, knowing that the ghosts were still howling somewhere out there. And knowing that if the monster or the bomb killed me, I would be out there with them.

But I had no choice.

And I had a really creepy feeling that the monster was very close. And waiting.

27

It wasn't that I'd just acquired a psychic power. The creepy feeling was just regular normal human intuition. Or paranoia.

Anyway, it was right.

But we didn't find that out right away. With the altered rock tucked under Sam's arm, we stepped off the Path and found nothing but the usual chilly, drifting swirls of mist.

'Seems we lost it,' Sam growled.

'If it's hunting us,' I said, 'it'll find us again.'

Sam nodded. 'No point waitin', then. Let's go and look for it.'

We set off once again across that eerie, lifeless land. I thought that I could just hear the shrill, breathy laughter of the ghosts, far away, but I might have imagined it.

Where we were, everything stayed as silent and empty as always.

But not for long.

'It's coming,' April said, her voice soft and shaky. 'Over there.'

'They made it a good tracker,' Sam muttered, as we looked where she was pointing.

Somewhere in the back of my mind that small vague scrap of a puzzling thought stirred again for an instant, but faded as the dark, dome-shaped monstrosity erupted out of the mists, slightly opened its huge mouth and surged towards us.

Wordlessly I held out my hand, and Sam gave me the bomb. It wasn't light, but I knew I could throw it far enough. My eyes met April's, and I wanted to say something but couldn't think what. So I settled for a half-smile, then turned and went to meet the monster.

It slowed slightly as it came at me, its lower edge rippling over the ground like long, horrible skirts. I stopped, waiting. Close up, it looked bigger than ever, and uglier. The big warty bumps on the front of it seemed to be pulsing in a revolting way. And the mouth opened even wider.

Staring into the dark cavern of that opening, I was pleased to see a definite lack of teeth. Just the faint sheen inside of some foul wetness.

Perfect, I thought. Open wide and hold that pose. I hefted the big rock, bracing myself to hurl it inside, hoping it would go in far enough. But while I was doing all that, the monster had other ideas.

Two of the ugly bumps above the mouth burst open. From them two long, thick, ropy tentacles flashed out, moving so fast that they whistled. Before I could even blink they whipped around me, binding me tight. Then they hoisted me into the air like a netted fish and slung me into the huge grisly cavern of the mouth.

And as the tentacles dropped me and pulled back and away, the mouth instantly closed around me with a fleshy slap.

The stink was worse than all the rat-infested sewers I'd ever known put together. Choking, half slipping on the slimy wetness that covered the inside of the mouth, I shifted the bomb into my right hand and drew the knife.

Sam hadn't said the word to explode the bomb, since I'd still been holding it. And the word wouldn't get through while the mouth was closed. So I had to put the bomb where it needed to be, then somehow try to force the mouth open.

But again, the magic guiding the monster got in the way.

From the floor of the mouth – glistening in the knife's glow – a writhing tangle of thin cords leaped up at me. As I tried to jump away, slipped again and fell, several of the cords wrapped around my legs.

But as other cords reached for the rest of me, I slashed at them with the knife. The blade sliced easily through several of them – and all the rest of them pulled sharply back, out of reach. Setting me free again.

Even better, all the flesh of the inside of the mouth rippled as if in a spasm of pain.

Sam had been right. The magic shielding wasn't protecting the monster's insides. Kannis or whoever had sent this creature had made the same mistake as Fray.

So maybe I could do the same thing too.

Of course this was a bigger mouth than the worm's. I had no idea where this thing's brain might be, if it even had one. It might be that the thickness of all that slimy flesh might keep the blade from reaching anything vital.

But before any new binding tricks came at me, I was going to try.

I sheathed the knife and raised the rock in both hands, thankful for its roughness in all that slippery slime. Heaving with all my strength, I flung it as far as I could into the darkness at the back of the cavernous mouth.

Then I yanked the knife out again and I swung around towards the front of the mouth. Slipping and sliding, gasping in the foul stink, tensed against some

153

new attack, I reached up and plunged the knife deep into the blubbery flesh of what would have been the inside of the upper lip, if the thing had lips.

The blade sank in as easily as a scalpel into suet. As I half expected, the monster heaved and jerked again, in a huge convulsion that almost flung me off my feet. Snarling, I stumbled sideways, ignoring the gush of reeking blood, dragging the blade along through the flesh, opening a long gash.

It's the reflex of any living thing. If it has something in its mouth that's hurting and stinging, it will want to spit it out.

The monster opened its mouth.

I got a flash-glimpse of April and Sam standing in the mists, looking horrified. '*Now!*' I screamed, and flung myself at the opening.

But I slipped in the slime again and fell, just as Sam shouted a strange rasping word.

With a ground-shaking ear-blasting noise like a colossal *whoomph*, everything around me went fiery scarlet. And something like a giant invisible sledge-hammer slammed into me and sent me flying into nothingness.

I came around with the usual flood of relief at finding that I was still solid, not a wraith wailing in the mists. As ever, by then there wasn't a mark on my solid self.

I'd even been cleaned up by April's magical laundry service.

And April and Sam were unharmed too, I was happy to see, though they looked a bit shaky as they peered down at me.

'I guess it was a good bomb,' I said, struggling up from the hard clammy ground. 'What happened?'

'April grabbed you with her PK,' Sam said, 'while I was sayin' the word to explode it.' He shook his head. 'It made a huge fireball, with gory chunks of monster flyin' everywhere, and the blast knocked us flat – and you came sailin' out of it as if you'd learned to fly.'

I reached a hand to April. 'Thanks – again,' I said. 'And for cleaning me up.'

'Any time.' She grinned.

Sam chuckled, patting me on the shoulder. 'You'd think the Cartel would just give up sendin' monsters, the way you keep killin' them off.'

'Not just me,' I said.

Then a bit wearily we turned back towards the Path. For a moment I thought happily of how furious Kannis was going to be, now that his monster had been turned into vanishing hamburger.

But happiness fled when I reminded myself that he'd now probably send – or do – something worse.

And meanwhile, somehow, we still had to find our friends . . .

155

28

We managed to retrace our steps to the Path with no problem. At once, as the power set us walking, we stepped off the Path again, to begin the random trial-and-error search process that was all we could do.

After walking a few steps into the mists, holding on to each other, we turned back on to the Path. Which looked exactly as bleak and endless and empty as it had every other time.

As we stepped on to it and began walking, April frowned. 'Can we really be *sure* this is a different part of the Path?'

I shrugged. 'All I know is what Bertrand told me,' I said. 'When you go off the Path, you always come back on at a different place.'

'Can you believe him?' she asked.

I shrugged. 'Not always. But he did warn us about the monster. And he'd have nothing to gain by lying about the Path.'

'I think we can be sure,' Sam said. He pointed at

something half hidden in the mists at the Path's edge. 'I noticed it before. Different rocks or bumps or dips on the ground, at different places beside the Path.'

'That would take even longer,' April said, 'looking at rocks and everything.'

'Maybe not if we look with ESP,' Sam said.

And with that, the wispy edge of a puzzling thought that I hadn't got hold of before came blazing full and clear into my mind and nearly knocked me over.

'Hang on!' I said. 'Why don't you use ESP to look at a *lot* of the Path, as much as you can? To see if you can spot Paddy and Julia on it somewhere?'

'It doesn't work, Nick, I told you,' April said, and Sam nodded in agreement. 'The Path blocks ESP.'

'But ESP works fine in the *mists*,' I pointed out. 'Bertrand found April and me, April sensed the monster, maybe even the monster used something like ESP to track us . . . And there's something else. When Bertrand told me about never being able to get back to the woman on the Path, who might be Julia, he said he wished his ESP was stronger. As if he believed that with more power he *could* have found her – by looking with ESP *at* the Path *from the mists*!'

It was like a comedy act, as their mouths fell open and their eyes widened in perfect unison.

'I never even tried . . .' April whispered.

'Nor me,' Sam muttered. 'Just assumed the Path would block it, like it blocks ESP when you're walkin' on it.'

'Try now!' I urged.

We went back into the mists at a gallop, but not too far in. There we stopped, Sam scowling in concentration, April's hazel eyes flickering with her power.

'You're right, Nick,' Sam said at last. 'I can see some of the Path. Looks just like the stretch we just left.'

'I can see the Path too,' April said. 'Quite a long bit of it. Totally empty.'

Sam nodded. 'You can see more of it than me because you have more psychic power. But we need to be able to see a *huge* long way along the Path, or else this kind of searchin' will be nearly as random as the other . . .'

He went quiet, a slow smile growing on his face.

'What?' April and I asked at the same time.

'There's a way to see more.' He grinned. 'We can scan *miles* of the Path all at once – if we link our powers together, April's ESP and mine!'

'Then what are you waiting for?' I asked.

April looked at Sam, waiting for instructions.

'Just take my hand and relax,' he told her. 'Try to sort of open your mind, and don't fight it. I'll make the link.'

So they clasped hands and turned to look in the

direction of the Path. I turned too, though I wasn't the one who'd be seeing things.

Except – I did see something. And so did they. But not something on the Path.

A movement, visible for an instant as the mists swirled, not far away. Something dark, rippling, flowing over the ground . . .

I reached for the knife, then saw that April and Sam didn't look troubled. They were just frowning at the spot where the flicker of darkness had vanished.

'Not another monster,' April said. 'It's that creep in the cloak, Bertrand . . .'

I scowled. 'Just what we need. He's probably disappointed that I'm still alive.'

'I wouldn't mind havin' a word with him,' Sam said. 'Skeleton or not, he's still a mage, and if he's been here a while he might know a few things.'

'He'll be around,' I said. 'He wants the knife, for some reason.'

But Bertrand had made himself scarce in the mists, so we forgot about him and got back to doing what we were there for.

Sam took April's hand again and did something psychic to make the link between their magical minds. April's eyes went wide and astonished – and almost at once they went wider.

'Sam, do you *see* . . . ?' she breathed.

'What?' I demanded.

'We're lookin' at more of the Path than I thought possible,' Sam said, sounding amazed. 'And I count eleven live people, at different places. Can't see too clearly, but one's sort of Julia's shape, and another walks a bit like Paddy . . .'

'Then let's go and look at them!' April said, eyes shining. 'It'll take no time at all! Not when we can see *exactly* where to find each one of them!'

29

We set off at a rush back to the Path, guided by their ESP to the person they'd seen who walked like Paddy – a slightly rolling stride, I remembered, head up and arms swinging.

But they hadn't seen that person in detail. Sam thought it was the magic of the Path still managing to get in the way a little. So when we came out on to the right bit of the Path, we saw that it wasn't Paddy. It wasn't even all human.

One of the Cartel's warrior creatures – powerfully muscled, in light armour like a Roman soldier, orange skin covered in stiff fur like briar thorns. With two gleaming fork-bladed swords that came whistling out of their sheaths when he saw us.

He didn't attack, but crouched, glaring. But of course the Path didn't let him stay still, so he kept walking towards us whether he wanted to or not. It might have been funny if he'd been a bit less scary.

As we took ourselves back to the mists, I was feeling

glad that he hadn't been one of the killers sent after me, in the past. And when April and Sam linked their ESP for another look, they seemed grimly intent on getting it right that time.

Instead they got something less scary but still not funny.

This time we went to find the one who looked vaguely like Julia's shape. Which turned out to be true only in terms of being thin. When we stepped back on to the Path we found ourselves almost on top of a scrawny, stooped, very old man, all long wispy white hair and wrinkly skin, wearing faded pyjamas.

He shrieked wildly at the sight of us and collapsed like a bag of bones, gabbling toothlessly. Begging us not to hurt him, as far as I could tell. But even then the Path's power kept the poor old soul moving, creeping painfully past us on bony hands and knees while watching us fearfully over his shoulder and still gabbling.

Since there wasn't anything we could do for him, we left him on the Path in whatever passed for peace, and went back into the mists for another try.

'I wish,' April said fiercely, 'that I had the power to put an end to this horrible place and send people like that *home*.'

'Have to put an end to the Cartel first,' Sam growled. 'But it's a good thought.'

Bracing ourselves, we started back to the Path to

look at the next one of the eleven people that their ESP had seen.

'Speaking of home,' I said to Sam, 'have you thought any more about getting us away from here? If . . . I mean, *when* we find Paddy and Julia?'

'I'm still workin' on that,' he said. 'There are lots of *translocation* spells, and some of them might be able to shift us back to our own world. I'm just not sure I've got enough power in me to make them work.'

'You mean we *can't* get away?' April said faintly.

'I didn't say that,' Sam growled. 'I've been thinkin' that I could maybe link your new higher magic with mine, April, as we did with our ESP, for an extra push. But there're still problems. Most translocation spells need a lot of special things, which we don't have. And one big spell that doesn't need that stuff *does* need a long complicated incantation and movements.' He grimaced. 'I'm not sure if I can remember every bit of it, word for word. Normally I'd read it out from a book.'

'But you have to *try*, anyway,' I said.

'Yeah, we'll have a damn good try. Nothin' to lose.' He sighed, then gave us a crooked grin. 'Of course, the Cartel sorcerers have some big magic already set up to move in and out of this realm. If Kannis shows up in person again, we could grab him and twist his arm, *force* him to take us home . . .'

It was a sort of joke, and April tried to smile. But I wondered – why not? If Sam and April together were strong enough to *grab* Kannis, I'd be ready to do some of the forcing. As I would have been with Fray. Giving rather than receiving, for once.

Though if they weren't strong enough . . . I decided not to think about that.

But there weren't any happy thoughts to take my mind off it. Because the third time we went back on to the Path, we found ourselves on another totally empty stretch. No one in sight anywhere. As if their ESP had gone suddenly wrong.

So we tried a fourth time, and a fifth time. And each time we arrived at a blank stretch of the Path with no one walking there.

'Must be gettin' twisted around somehow,' Sam growled. 'Or maybe the Path is confusin' our sight-lines . . .'

'What can we do?' April said.

'Keep at it,' Sam said. 'We found two of the eleven we spotted before. Only nine to go. Let's just keep our concentration steady.'

April nodded, but she looked close to tears with tension and disappointment.

And a few minutes later she did start crying.

But that was joy, not misery. Because the next time

we stepped from the mists on to the Path, we were looking at Paddy.

He went utterly still, staring at us with astonished disbelief. He looked as sturdy as ever, but his ginger hair
was thinner, his ginger beard had a few grey streaks, his
blue eyes had more lines around them. Those weeks on
the Path had left him as worn and rumpled as his jeans,
closer to looking defeated than I'd ever seen him.

And his jacket and shirt were still torn and scorched,
in front, from the flame that Redman had hurled on
that terrible day. Through the ruined cloth I could see
the silvery disc with a crystal embedded in it – the
powerful amulet that Sam had made, which had saved
Paddy's life.

As he stared at us he began to waver, as if the shock
of seeing us was affecting his balance. Or maybe it was
the sudden rush of joy. We weren't feeling all that steady
ourselves.

But still the Path kept him walking towards us – and
he managed a good try at a smile as April, in tears, flung
herself at him as she had with Sam. And when Paddy
also swung an arm around my shoulders too, my own
eyes blurred and a tear or two rolled down his cheek
into his greying ginger beard.

But he was also looking intently at Sam. 'What

about Julia?' he asked in that familiar gruff voice I'd thought I might never hear again.

'She's on the Path,' Sam rumbled. 'We'll find her.'

The relief of that nearly made Paddy's legs give way completely. 'I wondered if you'd find a way to come after us,' he said to Sam. 'Never thought you'd *all* come.'

'We got a free ride,' I said. 'Courtesy of a Mr Fray.'

That startled him, and got us away from hugging into talking, as we walked along. April and I finally had a chance to thank him and scold him for trying – hopelessly – to rescue us from Redman. But he said that once he'd found where we were, with psychic searching, he couldn't just leave us there.

'And Julia wouldn't let me go alone,' he said sadly. Then he shook his head fiercely as if to throw off the memory. 'Your turn now,' he said. 'Tell me what's been happening to you.'

So we gave Paddy a speedy outline of our adventures, before and after meeting Sam. And Paddy was hugely thrilled to know that April not only had her memory back but had turned out to be impressively magical in both ways.

'I bet Kannis is in trouble with the Cartel for that,' Paddy said.

'He got a little trouble from April too,' I muttered. April smiled. 'Nick said that it was funny how they've kept trying to mess up my mind and instead just woke up all these powers in me.'

'And then you messed *them* up,' Sam chuckled.

By then Paddy was looking a bit anxious and impatient about Julia. But he drew back when we started heading into the mists. He'd tried that once, he said, and as a psychic he suffered badly from the ghosts.

He relaxed though when Sam told him that the ghosts kept their distance from mages. So back in we went – linked in a line like a chain of paper dolls. Then Sam explained what he and April had been doing, and used his magic to bring all *three* of them together in a psychic link.

With the extra boost from Paddy's ESP they could see the Path much more clearly. It was as easy, and amazing, as that.

After rushing as fast as we could through the mists, towards a specific spot they'd seen, we stepped on to the Path again . . .

And there was Julia.

30

She must have been as totally astounded as Paddy had been, but she didn't make a sound or shed a tear. She just stopped as if she'd walked into a wall, stared at us, and silently fell on to her knees, head and shoulders drooping as if her last bit of strength had given way.

And when Paddy lifted her up and they stood in a fierce speechless embrace, Sam and April and I turned away, feeling like intruders.

Like Paddy, Julia looked worn and tired, thinner than ever, hunched and shabby in her cloth coat and jeans, her fair hair lank and tangled, dark circles under her eyes. Surprisingly though, for someone I'd known to be nervy and timid, she quickly began to gather herself.

But then, I remembered, she'd gone with Paddy on that hopeless mission to rescue April and me. And she hadn't seemed all that paralysed by terror even when they faced Redman.

More to Julia than I'd thought, I realized with a twinge of shame.

Soon we were all hugging again, as we had with Paddy. Julia clung to April and me for a long time, and she and April still kept arms around each other's waists while Sam started telling her about our adventures.

Julia flinched a bit when the story came to mention Bertrand Nowell. 'I *saw* him,' she breathed. 'He frightened me, and I just ran. He seemed so . . . creepy.'

'You're not wrong,' I muttered.

A moment later, when Sam got to the part where April found that she had the higher magic, Julia's pale eyes shone as if she personally had been given the gift. But when Sam was done, her eyes grew shadowed.

'I thought I'd be walking here forever, alone,' she murmured. 'But now we're all together, and with April's new powers . . . Sam, can you get us *home*?'

'With April's and Paddy's help,' Sam said cheerily, 'I think we have a chance.'

'Me?' Paddy looked startled. 'I'm just a low-level psychic!'

Sam poked him in the chest, grinning. 'I can link up with April's magic – and I can link with your *amulet's* magic the same way. I *made* it, I know how it works. And there's a translocation spell that should do the job – if I can remember all of it – with three of us to pump up the power.'

I felt a bit crushed, like a little kid not picked for a game. Once again I longed for some real power to offer. But even the knife wasn't like an amulet. It'd had magic done to it, as I had – but it couldn't *do* magic, and neither could I. So I'd just be an onlooker, like Julia.

And if some of that showed on my face, it was oddly enough only Julia who saw it, and gave me a small sympathetic smile.

But I did have some part to play, I discovered. Whatever spell Sam planned to try couldn't be managed on the move. We had to go back into the mists, away from the Path's power, so we could stand still. And in the mists, someone or something might be waiting.

'April and I will have to keep focused,' Sam said. 'Paddy won't, because it's his amulet we need, not his mind. So he can keep watch with his ESP. But we need you and Julia, Nick, watchin' our backs as well. In case the Cartel sends somethin' else to creep up on us.'

It was better than nothing, I thought. And I'd had a lot of practice at staying alert, through years of being hunted. For all I knew, Julia did too.

But when we got back into the mists, it all almost ended before it began.

The spell that Sam planned to use involved, as he'd said, a lot of words in the strange language of magic and special patterns being shaped in the air with hand movements. But it also needed a diagram to be drawn on the ground, for all of us to stand in.

That caused a brief panic, when none of us seemed to have anything to draw with. But at last Sam found the stub of a thick pencil in the depths of a coat pocket, and we all breathed again.

Then Sam spoke a word that cleared all the mist from the ground around us. Its surface, which I'd never seen so clearly before, was paler than the Path, just as hard, but more rough and uneven. Not the best drawing board. But Sam knelt down, brushed a few lumps of rubble aside, and started drawing.

The pencil line was vague and dim, and Sam had to pause twice so I could sharpen the pencil with the knife. Soon there wasn't much left of the little stub. But it was enough for Sam to draw three faint lines to make a neat and good-sized triangle.

'A triangle for our three sources of magic,' he explained.

Sam placed himself, April and Paddy at the three points of the triangle, while Julia and I got in the middle, back to back, to watch the mists. April was looking anxious, but Sam soothed her.

'Just relax and open your mind like before,' he said. 'I'll make the link with you and Paddy.' He gave us a half-grin. 'Don't worry. I've been goin' over the spell in my head, and I think I remember it all.'

I glanced at him uneasily. Could it really be as simple as that? I'd learned to mistrust things that looked too easy. And I would have been happier if Sam had sounded more confident, and if I hadn't seen the tension in his eyes . . .

Still, we all stood there quietly, waiting, hoping. And I could somehow *feel* the power rise around us, like silent electricity, as Sam's deep voice began. The spell seemed more complex than any I'd ever heard, long strings of words – some loud, some whispered, some sharp and harsh, some in a lilting chant almost like song. With endless hand movements making special patterns in the air.

Around us the mists drifted, and my nerves prickled and twitched as I stared at them, half expecting monsters or sorcerers to come stalking out. So I nearly jumped out of my skin when Julia suddenly gasped and clutched Sam's arm.

We all started to look wildly around, expecting to see some Cartel horror charging at us. But she was looking at a different sort of horror – at our feet.

That dire land didn't seem to like being drawn on. The thin pencil lines that made our triangle had completely disappeared.

31

'What now?' Paddy asked, his gruff voice hollow with despair.

Sam glowered at the tiny, useless scrap of wood that was all that was left of the pencil, then flung it away. 'We try again, use somethin' else to draw with.'

'We don't have anything else,' April said gloomily.

'What about blood?' I suggested. 'Paint the triangle with it. You can take mine, because I'll recover . . .'

But Sam was shaking his head. 'Good thought, Nick, but we can't. Only dark sorcery spells use blood. We might translocate ourselves to some demon realm worse than this.'

'Anyway, it might disappear too,' Julia murmured. 'We need a way to make a *permanent* mark on this ground.'

That started us all feeling dismal and hopeless again. But then another light went on in my head, and I startled them by laughing.

'Sorry,' I said as they stared at me. 'It's just . . . We *have* a way.'

And I drew the knife.

'I made a few gashes in the Path with it, when I first got here,' I told them. 'It didn't hurt the blade, and the marks faded away. But it was a good few minutes before they were completely gone. So if the triangle is cut deep enough, it could last long enough to finish the spell.'

'Then let's do it!' Sam said, holding out his hand.

I hesitated. The only two times anyone else had ever had the knife, it had been Fray holding it at my throat and Bertrand trying to steal it. But then, because it was Sam, I handed it over.

The blade's magic sharpness plus Sam's powerful arm soon carved a new triangle – several centimetres deep, glowing faintly – into the pale ground. Everyone took their positions, as before. Sam returned the knife to me with a solemn nod, took a deep breath – then again, slowly and intently, began the spell.

As it went on, the grooves in the ground grew shallower, slowly closing up. But the triangle was still faintly visible when Sam's voice died away and the spell was done.

Around us the silence seemed endless.

And nothing happened.

'That's all right, not to worry,' Sam said, trying for

a breezy smile. 'I must've said somethin' wrong or left somethin' out. I'll have a think, and we'll try it again.'

The rest of us were carefully not looking at him, or each other. Probably because the same disappointment and despair was filling them as they filled me.

'You said before,' April said, 'that some of those, um, translocation spells need special . . . *things*. Are you sure this one doesn't?'

Sam's smile faded. 'As sure as I can be,' he mumbled.

'Maybe there's not enough power,' Julia said, looking ready to scream or burst into tears. 'Sam—'

But Paddy put an arm around her and squeezed, which stopped her going on with whatever she was about to say.

'I don't think it's that,' Sam said. 'What we have should be more than enough.'

The silence returned then, and we stood watching the last bits of the triangle fade and vanish. Sam looked drawn and desperate, April's eyes glimmered with tears, Paddy and Julia were clinging to each other.

'I'm lettin' you all down and I can't work out how,' Sam growled. 'Maybe it's because of the magic in this place . . .'

And then we all went rigid at the sound of a different voice.

'Or perhaps,' the voice said, 'you simply need a little *help*.'

*

The lofty sarcastic tone was unmistakable. So was the dark, robed shape, as Bertrand stalked out of the depths of the mists.

The illusion of his face was intact, hiding the skull-grin within the hood. But even so he looked spooky enough to make Paddy glower, while Julia tensed even more.

'This is Bertrand Nowell,' I said. 'I'm not sure he's completely trustworthy – but he's not dangerous.'

Bertrand glared at me. 'You're more of a danger to yourselves,' he said nastily. Looking around at us, he barely glanced at Julia, raised an eyebrow at Paddy, gave April one of his odd searching looks, then turned to Sam.

'You're right though,' he went on, his usual smooth demeanour back in place, 'more power isn't what you need. Your problem is that you left out a rather crucial phrase in the incantation.'

Sam snorted. 'And you know all about it, do you?'

'I've memorized a great many spells,' Bertrand snapped. 'I always thought that translocation spells might be especially useful. Though I never expected to need one to get away from a place like this . . .'

'So *that's* why you tried to steal the knife!' I said. 'To draw the diagram!'

'Obviously,' he said. 'I could hardly do it with a fingertip.'

'Are you sure *you* remember the spell properly?' April asked.

'Quite certain,' Bertrand said. 'I have an *exceptional* memory, which as an actor I have trained and honed. In repertory theatre I was able to learn three separate roles at the same time, substantial parts, and play them alternately every week. All the lines, movements, entrances—'

'Then will you *help us*?' April broke in urgently.

'That's why I'm here, my dear,' he said, smiling at her.

'You mean you want to come with us,' Sam growled.

'Wouldn't you, in my place?' Bertrand said. 'My *body* is back there somewhere, in our real world. And even if I have to stay as I am, I want out of here. So we need each other, my friend.'

Sam still glowered, Paddy and Julia looked doubtful but April nodded.

'We could at least try it, Sam,' she said. 'I can sense that he's telling the truth.'

Makes a change, I thought. But I agreed with her. 'We're not going anywhere as it is,' I pointed out. 'Except back to walking the Path.'

So Sam agreed, a bit grudgingly. And I made sure that *he* used the knife, not Bertrand, to cut a new shape into the ground – a square now, to include Bertrand. Then Julia and I once again took our places inside the diagram, while the others each stood at one of the corners.

And Bertrand, in a clear, ringing, actorish voice, began the spell.

I was thinking, as I listened to him and watched the mists, how totally utterly awful it would be if some new Cartel horror chose that moment to launch another attack. But nothing like that happened.

Instead, as Bertrand spoke the last words with a grand echoing flourish, I felt something like a faint tremor under my feet.

In the next instant the mists vanished, and I was flying headlong through freezing, blinding darkness.

32

The feeling lasted for less than a second. Then I found myself on my feet, swaying and blinking in unexpected, unfamiliar brightness.

A patch of warm sunlight.

Pouring through one of the windows of the kitchen in Sam's house.

Around me the others were also blinking and staring, amazed and overcome, hardly able to believe what they were seeing. Paddy and Julia were speechlessly, wildly joyful, clinging to each other, suddenly laughing as if they'd never stop. And when April put her arms around me, we did some laughing and clinging too.

But Sam got busy. The instant that our feet had arrived on his kitchen floor he had waved his hands in weird magic gestures. Then he'd growled, 'Stand still,' before muttering a sequence of sharp rattling words.

Nothing seemed to happen, except for the faintest hint of haziness across the windows. But Sam breathed a great gusty sigh of relief.

'We should be all right now,' he said. 'Fray and the Cartel probably never imagined we'd escape the Path, so they didn't leave any tell-tales or booby traps here. And I've put a hideaway spell all around us, on the *inside* of the house – walls, windows, every bit. If Fray or Kannis or anyone does take a magical look, they'll still see an empty house.'

'Where's Bertrand?' April asked.

'Wherever he chose to be,' Sam answered. 'I made the choice for us to bring us all here, but he has magic of his own, so he'll have chosen his own place.'

'He's probably gone to try to find his body,' I said.

'Good riddance,' Julia muttered.

April peered at her. 'You didn't like him at all, did you?'

She smiled faintly and shrugged. 'He was just too creepy . . .'

'Still,' April said, 'we wouldn't have got here without him.'

'He'd better not get spotted by the Cartel,' Paddy said. 'They'd figure out that we're back too.'

'They'll probably find out before long,' Sam said, 'if they send somethin' else to hunt us on the Path.'

By then the sunshine was drawing us to a window. Gazing happily out at the real world, I felt I'd never enjoyed the sight of sky and trees and grass so much. Especially when it looked like we'd come back into an unseasonable warm spell, with the trees coming into leaf and flowers sprouting . . .

'Time moves differently on the Path,' Julia whispered. 'We've come back in the springtime.'

Paddy chuckled. 'But without being four months older.'

'I don't get older anyway,' I muttered.

'Lucky you,' Sam chuckled. 'Us greybeards, we're *happy* not to get older.'

We all laughed, though April seemed to give Sam and me an oddly thoughtful look. And I was thinking about the weird jump ahead in time that we'd made.

We hadn't had Christmas, I thought. I'd never got to buy, let alone give, April her present. But I suppose we also hadn't gone through winter in the city – all the flinty-grey skies, the clammy rain and sleet, the icy streets . . . the *mists* . . .

I never wanted to see a mist again in my life.

'Sam,' April asked, looking longingly out of the window, 'does your spell mean we can't go out?'

'We'd better stay inside for a time,' Sam said. 'A hideaway spell's not much good if you keep walkin' through it. We'll go out soon enough though. When we're ready.'

'Ready for what?' Paddy asked. 'War?'

'We've already got that,' Sam said. 'And we're not doin' badly. April has seen off Kannis once, Nick keeps killin' demons . . . What I want to do now is give April a crash course in the higher magic so she learns to *control* all that power. Then we might get Fray and Kannis off our backs for good.'

'The Cartel will just send others,' Julia murmured.

Sam shrugged. 'Maybe we'll find a way to reach some sort of stand-off. But meanwhile, I don't fancy just waitin' around to be attacked.'

Nor me, I thought. Been there, done that.

'Right then,' Sam said in a businesslike tone 'April and I have work to do. April . . .' he motioned towards the door, 'after you.'

So we settled into a routine. Paddy and Julia, never far apart, took over the chores and kitchen duties. Sam's magic reached into shops after they closed to bring clothes for the rest of us and food supplies – and April approved when he always left the right money in a till. And I spent those days enjoying something unusual, for me. Being peaceful.

I lounged around, read books, watched TV, gazed out of the windows at birds and occasional cats and people doing the normal things that ordinary people do. And I didn't feel bored for a moment. It was heaven. No ghosts, no demons, no dark magic looming out of coiling mists. Just springtime in the suburbs.

And I was enjoying watching April. She and Sam

worked long full days, but she ended every one of them bouncing and fizzing with excitement, thrilled with her crash course in the higher magic. And Sam was thrilled with her too, because she was an eager, hard-working student and a *very* quick learner.

'She's nearly got to a place,' he rumbled one evening, 'where she can go on learnin' by herself.' He grinned. 'Soon she'll be teachin' me.'

April laughed at that. But I'd seen what she had done against Kannis when her magic had been only a defensive reflex, unknowing and uncontrolled.

I wondered what she'd be able to do when she knew how.

In those days I started wondering about something else as well. A question that was never far from my mind whenever I had time to stop and think about anything. The question of Manta.

I still had no idea whether Manta was alive or not. When the Cartel took me prisoner, they hoped to tune in on one of the dream-visions she sent me and use it to track her. Maybe they had succeeded, and killed her. Or maybe she'd realized what they were planning and stopped sending the dreams.

Anyway, I was thinking more about Manta and April.

The more I pondered the few facts that I knew about

April's earliest days, the more certain I was that Manta could be her mother. But though I'd told April about the witch who made me changeless, I'd never so much as *hinted* about that possible connection. I didn't know how she'd react.

What I wanted, first, was to get her to try to remember more about her babyhood and her mother. And I wanted to talk to Sam about it, to see what he thought.

But, oddly enough, April herself raised the subject.

One morning she came to breakfast looking pleased and sort of wistful at the same time. Because of a dream she'd had – about being a baby in her mother's arms.

'I think some bits of my memory are still . . . coming back online,' she told us. 'And some got into this dream. It was really nice – though it was too vague . . .'

'How much did you see of your mother?' Julia asked, as I tensed up with eagerness.

'Her face was just a blur,' April said, which made me slump. 'But in the dream her arms were holding me close – soft arms that were strong as well. And her long hair was coming down over me like a curtain, all perfumed and tickly.' She sighed. 'The most beautiful wavy hair – like red gold.'

I sat up again, vibrating. That was it. That was *proof.*

I was quite sure that I'd never described Manta to April in any detail.

But then I saw Paddy looking at me with a small

frown. He'd laughed off my idea before, and I knew he'd be quick to point out that Manta wasn't the world's only redhead with blonde highlights.

So I said nothing. It was the wrong time, there at breakfast with everyone else around.

And the right time never came along.

Because a neighbour came knocking on the door.

33

It was the sniffy neighbour who had spoken to me after the attack by Fray's stone monster. Paddy and Julia and I watched him from a front window, knowing Sam's spell would keep him from seeing us.

Though he was dressed much as before, he looked different. Moving stiffly, as if he had a bad back, with a sort of empty look on his face. And after knocking a few times, he just stood there, blankly staring at the front door.

But at last he brought something like a rolled-up magazine from a pocket, shoved it part-way into the letter box and marched stiffly away.

Weird, I thought, as the three of us looked at each other and wondered what to do.

But then Sam came to see what the knocking had been. Looking annoyed by the interruption, he reached out – just as Paddy and Julia said 'Wait!' at the same time – and yanked the magazine all the way through the slot.

It was one of those giveaway catalogues from a mail-order firm. With a scribbled note from the neighbour saying that it had been delivered to him in error. All quite ordinary, even trivial.

But a disaster.

'Sam,' Paddy said, looking over his shoulder at the catalogue, 'there's no address on it. Why did he bring it *here*?'

And Sam swore and hurled the catalogue all the way across the room, looking furious and a bit sick, just as April came to join us.

'What's wrong?' she gasped.

'Me,' Sam growled. 'Bein' stupider than I can believe.' He stamped away, the rest of us following nervously. 'And now the Cartel most likely knows we're here.'

'How . . . ?' April breathed.

'They must've found out we left the Path,' Sam muttered. 'So I suppose they came sniffin' round here. And made my neighbour bring over a bit of junk mail, then not put it all the way through the letterbox.'

'And you pulled it inside,' Julia whispered.

'I *thought* your neighbour looked weird,' I muttered. 'Like a zombie.'

'You might've said,' Sam growled.

'You didn't give anyone a chance to say anything,' Paddy pointed out.

'Right. Sorry.' Sam looked even sicker. 'So anyone watchin' the house now knows somebody's in here.'

Paddy frowned. 'We can't know it's the Cartel . . .'

'I know,' Sam growled. 'But I've been here for years, and that neighbour's never done *anythin'* neighbourly before. From what Nick said, it sounds like he was under a command spell, and that means Cartel. So now they know someone's inside a house that looks empty. And they'll know *that's* a spell too. I'm really sorry.'

'We expected them to find us sooner or later,' April said.

'Yeah, well, I would've preferred later.' Sam gazed bleakly around at us all. 'Looks like our war is about to hot up again.'

Oddly though, nothing happened in the next few uneasy days and troubled nights. Paddy and Julia and I were never far away from one window or another. No longer enjoying the springtime, but keeping watch. And Sam and April spent even more time on her studies, increasing the pace. With April still thriving on it.

'She takes it in faster than I would've thought possible,' Sam told us one evening.

'That could be one of your psychic powers,' Paddy said to April. 'High-speed learning. Like you must have done when the Cartel had you.'

She had remembered that when she was their prisoner first, as a little girl, she got some schooling from a servitor and was also allowed to read whatever she wanted from the big house's library. Which seemed to have given her a better education than I ever had.

'The speed's just what we need,' Sam said. 'I think I could handle Fray, and I might even give Kannis a good fight. But with April, the way she's developin', we could see them both off.'

'Give us a demonstration,' I said idly to April.

She grinned. 'What do you fancy?'

But Sam held up a hand. 'Let's not. Save it for the Cartel.'

'If they're really anywhere around,' Paddy muttered. 'We've had no hint of it. I've been keeping a psychic lookout . . .'

'So have April and I,' Sam growled. 'But a high-level mage would know how to watch us without bein' spotted, and we've been caught out before.'

'But why would they be just *watching*, if they know we're here?' Julia asked. 'Why not just attack us?'

Sam shrugged. 'The Cartel often goes quiet when you expect them to come at you. Maybe they're tryin' to make us nervous – or workin' out a way to get at us – or puttin' some big evil magic together.'

Or all of the above, I thought.

But everything stayed quiet for another three days of

hard work for Sam and April, edgy watchfulness for the rest of us.

Then on the fourth day, at the earliest glimmering of dawn, some alarm rung by my survival instinct brought me suddenly awake. I came bolt upright, and lifted my pillow to look at the knife.

Its blade was lightly tinged with gold.

The fact that it wasn't fully luminous meant the danger was either not very big or not very close. And everything else in my dim and silent room looked normal. So did everything I could see outside when I crept to the window.

Just as warily, I got dressed and slid out of my room to rouse Sam and the others. But as I moved along the hall the knife suddenly glowed bright gold.

And where the top of the stairs should have been, I saw a different sort of opening.

A rectangle like a tall, clear window with rounded corners. Showing a view across a flat and empty landscape that stretched off to a hazy horizon. A lifeless place of bare earth, the dull reddish colour of old bricks, under a blank yellow sky.

As I stared the others came warily out of their rooms, also fully dressed, as if they too had been stirred up by some inner warnings.

But before any of us could say or do anything, the

190

impossible window suddenly expanded – swelling out towards us and all around us.

And took us away.

34

It wasn't like when we were taken to the Path. There was no sense of movement. One moment we were in Sam's carpeted hall, an instant later we were standing on that bare empty land, bathed in the sickly yellowish light from the sky, watching tiny swirls of reddish dust raised by a breeze that smelled musty and stale.

'Powerful magic,' Sam said, sounding calm.

'Can you do something?' Paddy asked.

'I don't know yet,' Sam said. 'I don't know what or where this is.'

'Another Cartel hell?' April whispered.

If it is, I thought, at least we'd all arrived together. And, as before, in one piece. Sam and April with their magic, Paddy with his amulet, me with the knife . . .

So we stood there and waited for the horrors. But what we got was a sudden shimmer in the air. Which became Fray, appearing as if through an unseen door.

Surprisingly, he was standing unaided, no sign of crutches or leg braces. His dark suit was as elegant as ever, his white hair and the rest of him was perfectly groomed as usual, his smile and his eyes looked as cruelly gleeful as before. And as insane.

'You must have thought you were *so* clever.' His voice was sharp and harsh, raw with the fury of his madness. 'Escaping from the Path, hiding and plotting in your little den behind your little spell.'

'While he's making his speech,' I muttered, 'could we just kill him?'

'Can't touch him,' Sam growled. 'It's an astral projection.'

Now that he'd mentioned it, I could just make out Fray's faint haziness. And that explained the restored legs. The astral thing is a sort of illusion, and illusions don't need crutches and braces.

I might have known Fray would play safe, I thought bitterly. He probably knows about April, and he wouldn't risk facing her and Sam together.

But I was sure that *something* would come to face us.

'I have proved my loyalty to the Cartel, sending you to the Downward Path. And once I have finished with you for good, they will see the error of their ways and return me to their magical fold . . . Especially now that it is *I* that have found you . . . your weakling actor friend may have gone straight to the Cartel to betray you in exchange for getting his body back . . . but it is *I* that have you!'

193

All our other feelings were suddenly buried in a burst of pure fury. It turned Sam crimson, turned April and Paddy white, made me snarl and Julia hiss.

'We should have *known*,' Julia muttered. 'Should never have trusted him . . .'

Fray laughed again. 'Oh, don't worry,' he sneered, 'The Cartel would never *honour* such a pathetic deal. The betrayer will be betrayed, you might say, and poor Bertrand will remain a skeleton. Mr Kannis will send him back to the Downward Path after tormenting him a while, I'm sure.' He bared his pointed teeth. 'And I will send your ghosts back, once I've had the pleasure of finally watching you die. Slowly.'

Sam's grin was savage. 'You just goin' to *watch*, Fray? Scared to try to do the job yourself?'

Fray stiffened, mad eyes blazing. 'Can you really think that a high-level mage of the Cartel would be afraid of *you*, Foss? You couldn't overcome me before, and you won't now. No doubt you have some power, since you escaped the Path. But you were helped then by your *friend* the actor, who is not here now. And two mere psychics and the boy will be no help to you here.'

Every one of us went very still, trying not even to twitch, as we realized what Fray had just said.

He didn't know about April. He thought she was still only a psychic, like Paddy.

Fray was still excluded from the Cartel, after all, so

clearly Kannis hadn't told him about her new higher-magic powers.

Sam was still grinning. 'If you're such a super-sorcerer, why haven't you got the guts to come here in the flesh and face me? One on one?'

The challenge mightn't have worked if Fray was sane. But since he was as crazy as a cockroach, it did.

He shrieked with rage like a toddler in a tantrum, and the faint haze vanished from around him.

The real Fray stood there on the red dirt, legs encased in metal braces, bright metal crutches supporting him.

'Come and die, then, fool!' he screamed, a fleck of froth on his lip.

'April,' Sam murmured, barely moving his mouth, 'make a mental link with me. When my magic hits him, you hit him at the same time.'

'Now, Sam, you said one on one,' Paddy said with a smile. 'That's cheating.'

'Absolutely,' Sam said. And he strode out to meet the enemy.

But the Cartel could have written shelves of textbooks about cheating. Especially Fray.

He began his horrible tittering laugh again. And as Sam moved forward, a squad of nine giant monster-warriors rose silently from the ground in a circle around him.

35

In the Cartel way, they were only partly human. They towered over Sam, their powerfully muscled bodies covered in purplish scales that glinted like shiny metal. Their heads looked like the heads of dinosaurs or dragons, scaly and hairless with small savage red eyes, jutting lizard jaws full of dagger-fangs, jagged metallic crests on their heads like oversized saws.

And their huge clawed hands held an assortment of ugly weapons – double-bladed axes, spiked metal clubs, short barbed spears.

As shock held us still for an instant, I wished uselessly for a good, big sub-machine gun, or a few hand grenades. But magic doesn't like machines. Guns wouldn't work in that non-place.

Sam's power, though, definitely did. The instant they appeared, the dragon-men struck at him, all at once. But they missed, because he was suddenly somehow outside their circle. Just as an enormous explosion went off *inside* it, a blast of magical energy.

But when the flame and smoke cleared, the monsters were still there, weapons raised, charging him.

'They're shielded,' April said, as if to herself. 'Though maybe not against everything . . .'

I saw her face tighten with fierce concentration, saw flecks of luminous gold flash in her hazel eyes. And then I had the demonstration that I'd asked for, before, of just how incredibly far she had come with the higher magic.

Suddenly we were all armed with long swords that glowed like the knife, weighing almost nothing. And our bodies were wrapped in a golden glow as well, which I knew was special shielding for us, weightless magical armour.

Sam had the armour and weapons too, a golden sword in each hand, roaring a battle-cry as he met the dragon-warriors' charge. And as we started towards him to join the fight, I saw that their shielding wasn't holding against those swords.

Sam flattened two of the monsters by the time we got into the battle, which then became more of a brawl. I had a high-speed glimpse of April swaying neatly away from a massive club while slashing at the clawed hand that held it. I saw Paddy's amulet as well as his shielding deflect a spear before he chopped down the spear-man like an ugly scaly tree.

At the same time I was paying attention to my own

problems. I didn't know much about sword-fighting, but I knew useful things about speed and balance and keeping cool. So just as one enemy bared his teeth in triumph when his strength twisted my sword out of my hand, his grin became an agonized grimace as the knife in my other hand took him in the throat.

In the same movement I dropped to the ground as a spiked club swept viciously through the space where my head had been. Rolling, I scooped up the sword and buried the blade in the club-wielder's scaly belly, then sprang to my feet . . .

There were no warriors left to fight. And Sam and April and Paddy were turning, with their red-dripping magic swords, to glare at Fray.

The sorcerer swayed for a moment on his crutches, looking shaken. But he was far from finished. He stretched a hand out towards us, starting to mouth an eerie phrase, his voice shrill and harsh.

And then I saw Julia.

She hadn't joined the fight, though she'd been armed and shielded like all of us. Instead, she had veered away, as if trying to escape the violence. But while we were fighting, while Fray was staring in dismay at the swift, brutal battle, Julia had been moving in a circle.

She had got behind Fray. And now she was running at him, wild-eyed, her bright sword poised.

It was crazily brave. And it should have worked. But

Julia was no athlete, and she wasn't running fast enough or quietly enough. Fray heard her. At the last moment he half turned with a snarl and flicked a hand in her direction.

An unseen force struck her as a hand might swat a fly, and hurled her away. Her flailing body flew high in an arching curve, then fell.

And the impact when she hit the ground made one of the most sickening sounds I've ever heard.

April cried out, Sam roared, Paddy yelled in anguish. But Fray's scream was louder – finishing the sorcerous spell he'd begun. And Sam's desperate shout, the start of some counter-magic, wasn't quick enough.

The nine dead or injured warriors vanished. And a small *army* of the same monstrous dragon-men rose up to take their place.

There must have been about forty of them. The shine of their purple scales was blurred, which probably meant they had even stronger shielding. And I knew that however many we killed, Fray would just make more.

'Do something!' Paddy rasped. 'I've got to get to Julia!'

Sam glanced at April, his face grim. 'We need a barrier,' he growled.

April nodded, clearly knowing what he meant. But as they started the chant and gestures to make whatever spell they were planning, the giant monsters roared like a herd of tyrannosauruses and charged.

I found myself stepping in front of Sam and April. I knew I couldn't stand alone against that charge. But I had the idea that I might at least get in the way, distract and delay the monsters long enough for Sam and April to do their magic.

Raising the knife and the sword, I braced myself against the horde of horrors thundering down on us.

But they never reached us.

The air was filled with a screeching, ripping sound, as if a sheet of metal was being torn apart like cloth. The monster army stopped in their tracks, held blank-eyed and motionless as statues. And suddenly, standing between them and us was a tall dark man in a long black coat.

A man with a blue-green devil-face.

Kannis.

36

He showed no sign of the knife wound I'd given him. And he seemed to be in a towering rage. His fangs were bared, his clawed hands clenched into fists, his eyes flared crimson. But as he stalked forward, I saw that his rage wasn't aimed at us.

He was going for Fray.

And I would have enjoyed going for *him*, again. But we were all held motionless by the same magic that had paralysed the warriors.

Totally confident in his power, Kannis didn't even look at us. 'Idiot, what do you think you're *doing*?' he raged at Fray. 'Playing some *game* with them? Don't you realize that all the girl's higher-magic powers are fully active?'

Fray, braced on his crutches, didn't flinch. 'I know that *now*,' he spat. 'And it's most strange. Foss surely lacks the power to free them. Could it have happened while she was on the *Path*?' He oozed sarcasm. 'Where you visited, did you not, *Mister* Kannis?'

'That's not important—' Kannis began quickly.

'No?' Fray interrupted. 'Was it also not important that *others* should be told?'

'The Cartel was told!' Kannis yelled. 'But you, fool, have been *excluded*! And you were *ordered* to abandon this crazed quest for vengeance! You were *directed* to leave these vermin to me! But again you disobey – and now you have blundered into this absurd battle, stupidly using *flesh-and-blood* warriors—'

'I have not blundered!' Fray screamed. 'I could easily finish them!'

'You could not!' Kannis snapped. 'You are too warped by your lust for revenge, too far out of control. From what I have seen, the girl has reached a high level, and has linked her power with the mage. Which is why I have come to end this.'

He raised his hands, muttering guttural words. The army of dragon-men vanished, and from where they had stood I saw streamers of dust rising from the hard ground.

The streamers gathered and whirled to form a circle around us. It then expanded, stretching high above us and down to the ground, so that it formed a circular enclosure of dust. Hanging there without sound, vibrating with eerie menace.

Then Kannis spoke a word and the reddish dust burst into furious scarlet flame.

*

202

It was magical, burning without fuel. But even so I could feel the blistering heat on my face as spiky tongues of flame licked out towards us, hungry and lethal.

'The fire will hold them,' Kannis said smugly to Fray, like a teacher giving a lesson. 'Now I can repair that unfortunate, ah, *accident* – and replace the barrier in the girl's mind, to stifle her magic again.' His fangs gleamed in a demon-smile. 'Then you may watch and learn, Fray, while I finally put an end to the others.'

He had turned back towards Fray, so he didn't see what I was seeing – and just as well. Sam and April were held fast by Kannis's paralysing power, but their *minds* weren't paralysed. And they were struggling furiously to free themselves.

Sam was sweating, red-faced, while April was deathly pale, her eyes blazing brighter than the encircling fire. As if the threat of a new blockage being put into her mind had sent her into a desperate frenzy.

But Kannis was still arrogantly confident that his prisoners were under control. And besides that, he was being violently, insanely distracted.

'You will *not* merely meddle with the girl's mind, you posturing clown!' Fray shrieked. 'She must *die*! If she has developed as you say, she is even *more* of a menace! The Cartel has tried before to contain her, and even then – without any of the higher magic – she was able to break free! It's how she did *this*, to *me*!'

He thrust out one metal-braced leg, like a kick in Kannis's direction. And the devil-faced sorcerer erupted with a fury that was almost as maddened.

'You call *me* a clown?' he raged. 'And you would *again* disobey a direct order? The Head of the Cartel wants the girl *alive*, you mindless fumbler, and so it must be! And if you get in my way, *you* will die as well!'

Truly foaming by then, Fray howled and struck at Kannis with a crutch. The bright length of metal magically stretched longer, slamming against the jaw of the devil-face with the sharp crack of breaking bone. Kannis swayed and cried out, then brought a glowing magical whip into his hand and lashed ferociously at Fray.

Despite everything, I actually started to smile a little, enjoying the sight of them flailing at each other like hysterical kids. But at once everything changed.

The sound wasn't much louder than snapping fingers. I barely heard it over the screeches of the two battling sorcerers. But somehow I knew what it was.

The sound of a magic spell breaking.

37

Suddenly we were free from the power that held us.
I staggered, and so did Sam and Paddy. But we
weren't looking at one another, or even at Fray and
Kannis.

Our astonished eyes were on April.

I had no idea how it worked, or what mages would
call the 'process'. Perhaps it was because of everything
that had happened to her in that dire place; perhaps it
was a link with Sam's magic. But clearly her powers had
been lifted to another level.

She put the golden shielding back on to us, and gave
us back our bright swords. But she found something
different for herself. Her astonishing power reached out
not to quench Kannis's circle of flame but to *gather* it.
Suddenly it was swirling and flickering around her,
clothing her like a fiery robe.

I thought of how Manta, in a dream-vision, once
called April 'the stormchild'. And I'd seen a few storms

that April had made. But now I truly saw the awesome extent of her new powers – and her wrath.

Like an avenging goddess, like a small blazing sun, she lifted smoothly up from the ground. Her hand collected a portion of her robe of flame, shaping it into a long, pointed, fiery spear. More like a thunderbolt, when she hurled it.

By then Kannis and Fray were staring at her in wild shock – and with some fear as well. But they hadn't become helpless, and they'd never been weak. As the flame-spear blazed towards them, they got some magic in the way to block it. Kannis was only staggered by the impact, though Fray half fell as one leg gave way.

Seeing that stirred the rest of us into action. Sam in his golden armour moved towards April as if to reinforce her, though I wasn't sure she needed it. When the two sorcerers struck back with a ferocious blast of their own fire, it just curved harmlessly past April and Sam and vanished.

It missed Paddy too, because he was scrambling towards Julia where she still lay, motionless. And the blast went nowhere near me, because I was also moving.

Gripping the knife, with the golden sword in my right hand, I was running flat out. Aiming to do what Julia had tried to do. Aiming for Fray.

*

He was still struggling to his feet, while Kannis was shrieking with what sounded like desperation as well as fury as he formed another barrier against another flaming bolt from April. So I almost made it.

But when I was only a few strides away, Fray sensed that I was there as he had sensed Julia. With a startled shriek he whirled, swinging one of his crutches at me.

The crutch magically became a long, vibrating blade, murderously sharp. As it flashed towards me I swung the sword – deflecting the blade but shattering the sword. Before Fray could strike again I dived forward and drove the glowing knife at his heart.

But panic and madness had speeded him up too. He lurched wildly backwards, and my lunge over-extended me, throwing me off balance. So the knife missed his heart and sank into loose flesh on one side just above his hip-bone.

He screeched and fell, almost dragging the hilt from my hand. I stumbled as I fought to jerk it free. And Fray, screeching and bleeding, struck out again with his long blade. It was aimed at my head, and I flung my right arm up to block it. The blade sank into my fore-arm, shearing through flesh and bone. My scream of pain echoed Fray's – but he was frantic and foaming, made crazier than ever by pain and fear. And I could handle pain.

In that instant I had an edge-of-vision glimpse of

April rising higher into the air, still in combat with Kannis, her hair streaming out around her as if she'd been electrified. The sight was just what I needed to help me stay focused.

Sprawling on the ground, trying to wriggle away, Fray still clutched the vicious blade. Fallen on to my knees beside him, blood spurting from my severed arm, I raised the knife high, determined to kill him whatever he did.

But both Fray and I were thrown off balance again when the ground shook under us all as if an earthquake had struck.

April's power had split the earth itself, opening a huge deep cleft under Kannis's feet. With a high, thin scream the devil-faced sorcerer toppled into the gap, which closed around him like a devouring mouth.

But he was still Kannis. The earth rumbled again, and he rose up out of it, his devil-face even darker with new fury.

As shock and blood loss began blurring my vision, as the long vibrating blade fell from Fray's weakened hand, I saw that instant poise itself in an eerie silence. April and Sam were raising their arms, building a new onslaught, while Kannis gasped a spell to protect or counter-attack.

And with the last of my strength I lunged at Fray, raising the knife again.

But I didn't get to him. And in the other battle the spells were never finished.

The blast that shattered that moment of silence, and flung me back into a pool of my own blood, made April's thunderous blasts of power seem like whispers. It sounded and felt like the colossal cosmic explosion that might spell the demolition of a world.

And with it came a monstrosity, seeming to fill the sky.

It was an immense bodiless head, the size of a three-storey house, with a more or less human face. Corpse-grey skin, matted white hair and beard, bulging volcanic-red eyes with facets like giant rubies, a mouth like a vast, lightless cavern in the depths of hell.

And when it spoke, the thunderous voice seemed to shrivel my soul.

'DID YOU IMAGINE I WOULD NOT *NOTICE* THIS FOLLY?'

It was clearly talking to Fray and Kannis, who shrank and cowered. And in the same instant April and Sam and Paddy were totally, helplessly enclosed, in three long transparent boxes like coffins made of glass.

And then they disappeared.

'No, no, you must not, you *will not*! They are *mine*!'

The choked screech came from Fray, struggling to his feet, ignoring me, ignoring his own dripping wound. Eyes staring and face contorted, he looked more insane than ever. And proved it by launching a stream of lurid fire at the colossal head in the air above him.

The fire simply vanished. And the earth shook as the Head spoke again.

'ONCE AGAIN, MUTINOUS ONE, YOU HAVE GONE TOO FAR,' it thundered. 'YOU WILL GO NO FURTHER.'

And Fray simply exploded, noisily, into red spraying fragments of flesh and bone.

I was close enough to get some of the impact of that explosion. It flattened my damaged body where I lay, with a new flare of agony. Unable to scream or even breathe, my vision blurring, my blood gushing, I plunged into darkness.

And never felt the landing.

38

With a severed arm I should have bled to death too quickly to be restored. Especially after whatever extra damage came from Fray's explosive death. So I was more hugely astounded than I'd ever been to wake up alive and back to normal.

And I was astounded all over again to find myself lying on the carpet of Sam's hall at the top of the stairs.

When my eyes opened I just lay there till my nerves stopped vibrating. Then I lay there for a while longer, feeling empty and shattered, wishing that I'd never woken up at all.

I knew beyond doubt that the terrible monstrosity of that head had been just that – the Head. Of the Cartel. And my mind kept replaying the image of April and Sam and Paddy, trapped in glassy coffins by the Head's gigantic unbelievable power.

Wherever they'd been taken, they were prisoners of the Cartel again. And I wasn't in much doubt about what would happen to them.

Sam and Paddy might already be dead.

And though the Head apparently still wanted April kept alive, I knew it wouldn't care about keeping her *intact*.

I'll never see her again, I thought. And those words made me feel more miserably lost and alone than I'd ever felt in my lonely life. Worse even than when I landed on the Path.

But I didn't scream and weep and go berserk as I had then. I just lay there. In a while, I thought, when I'd found a bit of will and nerve, I'd get up and get on with the hopeless process of looking for her.

I didn't have a clue where to start, but that didn't much matter. I couldn't really hope to find her, when she'd been swept away to an unknown horrible somewhere by the mind-wrenching, soul-twisting power of the Head of the Cartel.

I guessed that the only reason I hadn't been put into a glass coffin was because I'd looked dead. And I could also guess at how long I'd last, once the Head learned that I'd survived.

That grim thought stirred me enough to start the process of getting up. But I'd barely moved when a voice behind me almost stopped my heart with shock.

'They think we're dead, you know,' the voice said.

A toneless voice that sounded as bleak and empty as I felt. A voice I knew well.

I sat up and turned to see Julia sitting against the wall, watching me.

'I thought you *were* dead,' I gulped.

'I nearly was,' she murmured. 'But I think, even in the midst of that terrifying battle, April had the power to reach out to me and heal me.'

'So you saw what happened . . .' I began.

She flinched a little, probably seeing those glass coffins again in her mind, as we both would see that whole scene for however long we lived.

'Up to when Fray died,' she said after a moment. 'Of course it had been Fray's magic that made that place and took us there. So when he was killed, his spell was broken, the place vanished – and you and I came back here.'

'I would've liked to finish Fray off myself,' I muttered.

'You had a good try,' Julia said.

'We both did,' I said. 'I think what you did surprised everyone.'

Her mouth twitched in a bitter half-smile. 'It wouldn't have surprised Paddy.'

I nodded vaguely, getting to my feet, sheathing the knife that was, amazingly, still in my hand. Then I

213

realized that a large piece of my shirt was missing, and saw it on the floor, red and sopping wet with blood.

'I used that and a lot of pressure to slow your bleeding,' Julia said. 'To give your healing time to work.'

'Thank you,' I said. It wasn't much of a response, after she'd saved my life. But we were both too drained and numb for anything else.

I was vaguely aware that life was going on outside in ridiculously normal ways – spring sunshine through the windows, a gentle breeze, happy birdsong. But my mind was still clogged with loss and desolation, with memories of terrible sights and a deafening thunderous voice from the sky . . .

'That *was* the Head of the Cartel, wasn't it?' I asked.

'I imagine so,' Julia said, empty-voiced.

'Wouldn't mind having a try at him too,' I muttered.

I was shocked again when Julia laughed. Not the nervous giggle that was normal for her, but a sharp-edged sound that cracked like a whip.

'Put it out of your mind, Nick,' she snapped. 'And forget about dying in some final heroic battle. Manly posturing isn't what we need.'

I stared. She was still thin, pale Julia with straggly blonde hair, but she wasn't washed-out, timid Julia any more. Her light-blue eyes held a hard sapphire glint, and her small chin was set like granite.

'What *do* we need?' I asked warily.

She rose to her feet, her blue stare fixed on me. 'I don't believe Paddy and April and Sam are dead, Nick. I *won't* believe it. And you shouldn't either.'

'All right,' I said, frowning.

'So our first and only objective,' she said, 'must be to get them back.'

That made me wonder if all the horrors had unhinged her mind. 'Just the two of us?' I said. 'Against that Head and the rest of the Cartel? Do you have some magical super-powers that you've kept hidden? Because I haven't.'

'Don't be silly,' she said. 'You may have no magic of your own, but you've been damaging the Cartel for years. The two of us together can do even more. We can get a long way before they even realize we're coming.' Her eyes flashed, looking fearless and determined. 'And we're not going to *fight* them. We're going to sneak around and be crafty and clever – and find a way past them.'

She turned briskly away, as if to start getting ready for the journey. But I stood still, amazed by this new, tough Julia. She'd take some getting used to.

Then I grimaced and shrugged and followed her.

Whether we got anywhere or not, and however sneaky we were, I knew that before too long the Head, or Kannis, or some Cartel psychic would notice us.

Then they'd simply wipe us out, like brushing lint from a sleeve.

But that thought brought me no flinch of fear, no quiver of horror. I was beyond all that. At least, I thought, I'd have company along the way. So let's give it a try.

Get as far as we can before they find us.

Do as much damage as possible before we fall.

Find our friends . . . or die trying . . .

*Look out for the final bloodcurdling instalment of the
DEMONS TALKERS trilogy, coming soon . . .*

DEMON STALKERS

VENGEANCE

Douglas Hill

'You're a legend Nick, you're a warrior now . . .'

Nick Walker, the Changeless Boy, must journey to the
very heart of the Cartel – an organization with evil and
brutality at its core.

But once he arrives, nothing is as it seems – faceless
beings are farmed for food by insect henchman, and
Nick's friends have been transformed into soulless
slaves who want him dead . . .

A selected list of titles available from Macmillan Children's Books

The prices shown below are correct at the time of going to press. However, Macmillan Publishers reserves the right to show new retail prices on covers, which may differ from those previously advertised.

Douglas Hill

Demon Stalkers: Prey	978-0-330-45214-4	£5.99

E. L. Young

S.T.O.R.M. – The Infinity Code	978-0-330-44640-2	£5.99
S.T.O.R.M. – The Ghostmaster	978-0-330-44641-9	£5.99
S.T.O.R.M. – The Black Sphere	978-0-330-44642-6	£5.99
S.T.O.R.M. – The Viper Club	978-0-330-45416-2	£5.99

Elizabeth Laird

Secrets of the Fearless	978-0-330-43466-9	£5.99
The Garbage King	978-0-330-41502-6	£4.99
A Little Piece of Ground	978-0-330-43743-1	£4.99

All Pan Macmillan titles can be ordered from our website, www.panmacmillan.com, or from your local bookshop and are also available by post from:

Bookpost, PO Box 29, Douglas, Isle of Man IM99 1BQ

Credit cards accepted. For details:
Telephone: 01624 677237
Fax: 01624 670923
Email: bookshop@enterprise.net
www.bookpost.co.uk

Free postage and packing in the United Kingdom